Out of the Whirlwind

Out of the Whirlwind

M. T. Kelly

a novel

Published in 1995 by
Stoddart Publishing Co. Limited
34 Lesmill Road
Toronto, Canada M3B 2T6
Tel. (416) 445-3333
Fax (416) 445-5967

Stoddart Books are available for bulk purchase for sales
promotions, premiums, fundraising, and seminars. For details,
contact the **Special Sales Department** at the above address.

Canadian Cataloguing in Publication Data

Kelly, M. T. (Milton Terrence), 1946-
Out of the whirlwind

ISBN 0-7737-2901-1

I. Title.

PS8571.E5508 1995   C813'.54   C95-931150-5
PR9199.3.K4508   1995

Cover Design: Bill Douglas/The Bang
Text Design: Tannice Goddard
Printed and bound in Canada

Carl Schaefer's "Rocks, Pickerel River, 1993," courtesy
of Penumbra Press, *Twelve Northern Drawings*.

*Stoddart Publishing and the author gratefully acknowledge the support
of the Canada Council, the Ontario Ministry of Culture, Tourism,
and Recreation, the Toronto Arts Council, Ontario Arts Council,
and Ontario Publishing Centre in the development of
writing and publishing in Canada.*

For
Alex Hall
Fort Smith
NWT

"Then the Lord answered Job
out of the whirlwind"

Job 38:1

Contents

Out of the Whirlwind

I

Rapids of the Drowned

The river had swallowed a house, and the whole town had been moved back, again. The gap where the bank gave way was as big as a quarry, crisscrossed by the trails of dirt bikes. Now his father, standing on the second-floor porch of the store, could see unhindered right across the Slave to the far side; he always came out to watch the sunsets. But he would be inside at this time of the afternoon; no one seemed to be travelling on the streets of Fort Smith.

Billy, who was walking, ducked into the Anglican cemetery. The space was filled with sun which spun off the wings of mayflies. As the insects lifted, Billy felt he could see through the spruce that walled off the clearing, see right through to the open, active part of town now bright with new green, the spring green of the prairies. But it was July in Fort Smith.

There it was: "A Good Cook" in lead letters in marble. And a nickname, "Cliff." Nothing else. The shock on seeing it never quite went away. When they'd first moved here and he'd discovered this place and that gravestone, it expressed in a blunt way so much that made him uneasy about the North. He'd been alone, and there was in that cry — for the epitaph felt like a cry to him, in spite of its bravado — distance and uselessness, as if nobody should ever have come into the country. It was about silence, white people, for the natives didn't seem to affect the quiet the same way; it was like the old-timers' word *lonesome*. "A Good Cook" came from a still camp on the afternoon of a sunny day like this one, three words and nothing else against the high blue wilderness sky.

That was years ago, but he could still feel he belonged in Alberta. Always in summer; nothing to do. The trail from this clearing offered a gentler, more hidden slope down to the Rapids of the Drowned. He didn't go down there anymore.

Leaving, Billy passed the little grave with the carved pickets. Made of plywood, the laminates were finally separating. When he'd first seen them they'd been new. A pair of baby booties dangled on the side of the plot, the shoes' white leather almost paper from so many winters outside. Blackflies were beginning to bother him, and he didn't stop.

At home he found his father in costume. "Big Bill" Bonnicastle was under six feet, but when he wore his black Stetson with the feather, his buckskin shirt with the beaded floral patterns, his cowboy boots, he looked taller. Behind his hornrims were black moist eyes that seemed both expressionless and too sensitive at the same time.

"Listen, son," the old man said, and Billy was instantly uncomfortable. All his life he'd been uncomfortable when his father called him son. When he was little he kept protesting it was stupid. He couldn't say why he hated it, but the resentment flared again and he barely heard his father continue.

"There's some people I want you to meet. They're upstairs."

Aside from being called son, Billy was angry because his father seemed to be making an announcement. Big Bill had a twinkle of performance in his eye. He was talking for himself and an audience, telegraphing the punchline to a folksy joke, though there was no one there but Billy. That didn't seem to matter.

In the living room were two strangers. They sat together on the edge of the sofa looking afraid they'd knock something over, both of them big in the small room, their legs turned away from the coffee table. Papers and maps had fallen off the table onto the floor. The woman was dark, with tanned legs in dark stockings, white spots showing on her knees because her legs were tilted so far back they were nearly tucked under her. She could have been native. Black hair cut cleanly across her face, down to thin lips and bright lipstick. Her dark complexion made her eyeshadow seem soft, and there were sparkles in it. Tilting her head, she looked at Billy in a friendly, poised, slightly curious way, but it was also as if she didn't quite see him. She did not speak.

The man was very tall, with a small head. His strange dark red hair was long on top, plastered down. He wasn't hiding a bald spot, he just had fine hair, and small features, a little ski jump of a nose. As Billy's name was spoken the man glanced furtively at the mantelpiece, worried a figurine was about to fall and he was the one who'd bumped it.

"Hi," Billy said.

Big Bill, with a piratical grin, reached for an

7

envelope on the mantel. He did knock something over, a porcelain statue, which fell and
didn't break. It seemed they'd all been waiting
for it to happen. "Damn." Big Bill lost his grin,
but quickly reverted to it, ignoring the floor.

With the envelope at arm's length, and nearly
waving it, Billy's father proclaimed, *"JOURNAL
of a Journey with the Chepawyans or Northern
Indians, to the Slave Lake, & to the East & West
of the Slave river, in 1791 & 2, by Peter Fidler."*
With his other hand, in an awkward gesture, he
pushed his glasses up the bridge of his nose.

The other people in the room stared at the
ceramic maiden in sun bonnet lying on the rug.
The guests strained toward it, but couldn't
move to pick it up, as big and trapped as they
were. Billy turned to leave.

"I'm Malcolm." The tall man smiled. He had
gaps in his teeth. His voice was completely
unlike his appearance, welcoming and assuring,
the voice of someone who loved to talk, who
made things interesting. "This is Claire."

"This is where you should go, eh." Billy's

father held out his document. "You should read it." He turned to Billy. "They have a trip planned for the Barrens, and they'll need some help."

The woman didn't say anything. Her red lips got tighter, but it wasn't a smile.

"It's got the Dog River in it, the Salt, where I have my cabin, the Little Buffalo, the Talston," Big Bill continued. "Nobody in Fort Smith knows about this!"

"I know you love it," Malcolm said.

"Damn right. It's my home."

"But sometimes that mighty river can seem a mudhole."

"In spring, maybe," Big Bill said.

"July's spring in the tundra." Malcolm seemed to regret calling the Slave a mudhole.

The rictus of his grin grew harder as Big Bill hung on to his territory. "The Slave is none too popular around here because" — he grew crafty, let them in on a secret — "it was a civil servant's house that went down last time. Gov'ment don't like to be stood up to. Okay, everybody move back, whole town move back! Hell, that house was too close from the beginning."

"Pardon?" Claire said.

"The riverbank collapsed and took a house with it," Billy said. "The bank's unstable. It's happened before."

"There isn't much sediment in those clear northern rivers," Malcolm said with good humour. "Not even in runoff."

"There's not much of anything," Big Bill grunted.

"They're clear," Malcolm said.

Claire lost her absent look and smiled at Billy, though he still didn't think she saw him. She seemed about to say something when Big Bill broke in again.

"Well, you know the young lad," he said.

Malcolm laughed. "I don't know him. I've heard of him." Again, the voice was startling. The transformation from an ungainly man, uncomfortable with his body, to someone Billy really wanted to know was uncanny. He should-n't have a name like Malcolm, Billy thought.

"Hi," Billy said again.

"We've got a long summer planned," Malcolm explained to Billy, "and I'm fantasizing about an overwintering, though we've left things late."

There was silence, surprise. Fear, disaster, stupidity suddenly attached to Malcolm's words: "overwintering," "left things late." The very tone of his voice had changed as he said them: stubborn.

"Winter." Big Bill hung his head. "I don't know."

"Overwintering?" Claire frowned. "What are you talking about!"

"I said 'fantasized,'" Malcolm tried to joke, and quickly turned away from Claire. "It's hard to get anyone to go on these trips," he said to Billy.

"I haven't been to the Barrens," Billy said.

"I don't like that word." Malcolm pursed his lips. "I like *tundra*."

"'With no provisions, no tent, scanty clothing, and hardly any ammunition, Peter Fidler, at the age of twenty-two, set out to live with the

11

Indians for the winter,'" Big Bill read from his papers. "They were near Fort Smith, they were at the mouth of the Talston, and the country they roamed through had a very limited supply of fish or game. The climate's one of the most rigorous in the world." Big Bill paused. "Though that may be overdoing it."

Claire smiled. "It's the subarctic."

"I never think of it that way living here," Big Bill said, "though we've been called the mosquito capital of the world."

"You can't stay out on the tundra for the winter," Billy insisted, speaking quickly and feeling more alarmed than he should have.

"He said 'fantasizing.'" Claire looked pointedly at Malcolm as she spoke.

Billy rushed out what he had to say. "The Thelon's a game sanctuary. You need a licence. You can't cut down trees in the Oasis. There's nothing there. There's nothing to eat."

"I know," Malcolm laughed. "We're going on a summer canoe trip. But it will be a long one, and as your dad said, we need some help."

"Well, I wrote you about your route," Big Bill said. "By God."

Now he's going to go on about my not having a summer job, Billy thought, but Big Bill just nodded, congratulating himself.

"Right," Claire said. "Well, you didn't write me that Fort Smith was the mosquito capital of the world."

"Why, we'd never met," Big Bill said, looking about to bow. "I didn't know you were coming. We're distinguished by our mosquitoes."

Would he throw in "my dear lady"? This courtliness made Billy sick. His mother paid no attention to it, but it made him sick.

Then Big Bill became serious and admitted, "It *has* been a bad year for mosquitoes."

"Right," Claire said again, looking odd and troubled.

The strange, calm look Claire had, her face not frozen but the expression held so tightly it seemed too still, confused and enthralled Billy. She wasn't stupid; she wasn't serene. With her head tilted, not quite in a questioning way, on the verge of being puzzled, she irritated and intrigued him. She gave nothing away, yet she wasn't detached. Now she was frowning; he didn't want her to frown.

"The wind needs to blow," Billy said. "That's all. Then there's no more mosquitoes. It'll blow on the Barrens."

"It's the wildlife we want to see," Malcolm said. "The animal nations."

"Well, you're going at the right time," Big Bill said. "There's July, and then there's the rest of the year."

II

Land of Feast and Famine

The Barrens, and her anxiety, did not change in the rain and wind. Here the river widened, and banks of sand that had seemed unbelievably white in the sun still dazzled under a low sky. Behind her tent, which overlooked the great breadth of the Thelon, were hills. They seemed part of a huge body she could actually touch, which was endless. Claire shivered and thought about caribou crossing, small and far away, down where molten light would touch the water in August, fall. The wind blew so hard the rain struck her horizontally.

"There's a chipping site near my tent." Because of the gale, the flapping and creaking tent, she hadn't heard Malcolm come up behind her and she jumped. "You'll get wet," he said.

Turning away, hugging herself, Claire suddenly felt deep fatigue, though she'd slept through the morning.

"It could blow and blow," he said. "But we'll travel tomorrow."

When she didn't answer, Malcolm threw out his arms with that crazy, abrupt exasperation of his and stalked away. It was getting worse, or at least he never made an effort to change. Looking down at her boots in the spongy tundra, Claire automatically searched for wildflowers. Soon Malcolm was on the shoulder of a hill, his blue jacket moving against the strewn, broken stones of the crest.

The strangest thing of all about these Barrens, stranger than anything she'd experienced, was how, not familiar, but natural it seemed to be there. The clear, still edge of tundra ponds, a yellowlegs' cry in the wind, no other people, the cold, all hinted at some deep order, reassuring yet impersonal.

How different was this scudding, squally sky — big and lit from the inside — this clamorous wind, from that morning when Malcolm had come up to her outside the biology building and started all this. Half a year ago, November. Now she was here.

In his long, wet coat, standing on the steps, red hair wet across his forehead — it was such a strange colour it looked as if there was henna in it — he hinted at the kind of complete preoccupation that was a warning: eccentric, mad. Already the security guard was watching him from the vestibule. Malcolm wobbled his head; his lips were mobile.

Claire came out into the still misty lunch hour and carefully looked beyond him, across the street to the soggy lawn, the concrete gazebo over the time capsule buried by the library. The huge windowless wall rose up, lost in cloud, and she felt she was daydreaming; she forgot all about him and then he spoke.

"Don't you have access to the lab?" His accent was strange, one she couldn't place: articulate, overeducated, someone in second-hand clothes from a chess club. He mumbled a figure and dropped her boss's name, mouthing the words as if they were marbles in his mouth, ready to listen to his own analysis and saliva. Fleetingly, she wondered if he was schizophrenic.

"Pardon?" she said. Access, she thought, he wants access, which could be more than trouble. He could be dangerous.

"You work for Daryl, don't you?"

His voice changed timbre, which confused her. He still seemed eerily intelligent, but the way he pronounced Daryl's name implied he was standing up for her in some way. Claire didn't know what to say, lifted her chin in a way people took as haughty, and stared off to the side.

"I'm not a friend of his, but I know who he is," Malcolm said candidly.

His presentation of self had changed utterly. The way he spoke was so warm, so reasonable, and the obvious, the ordinary, seemed startling, new. Trying to stay suspicious, Claire was completely surprised. It was only reasonable he should have a hearing. She wanted to listen to him talk.

"How do you know him?" she asked.

"Do *you* know *The Fallacy of Wildlife Conservation*?" Malcolm asked her back.

He was one of those people, she thought, and snapped "No" back at him, breaking her rule not to engage.

"Wait a minute, take it easy," he said.

"Would you rather your child had a kidney transplant or that some rat lived? That's what you're on about, isn't it?"

"I don't have any children," he said in an unusually calm way.

"If you break in here you'll go to jail."

"You're right, that is what I'm on about, but it's not what you think."

"No?"

"I don't mean to address the whole issue of access, letting the public in..."

She could smell the wet wool of his coat. What a depressing day. "I have to go work out."

"I'll come with you."

"No you won't!"

"Really. I don't mean to... This *is* important."

"Who are you?"

"Malcolm. I'm doing a piece for *Animal Voice*."

"No kidding."

"I do have an open mind," he said calmly. "But nobody can get in and —"

"That's right."

"I want to know about the lab. Not even the conditions. I just want to see one. We hear all these reassurances from you guys, from panels of vets, but nobody can get in."

"The conditions are good."

"Look, this is the institution that gave the

world the image of the engineer in the white coat eating a DDT sandwich to demonstrate it couldn't do any harm."

She had to smile. "It probably didn't do him any harm."

"Can I talk to you? I know you have the best hands at U. of T.," he tried to joke, "in Canada."

She really was good at what she did, those tiny, tiring operations — but his flattery didn't change her mind. There was that promise in the way he talked to her, of insight, a different light on what she already knew, energy. And she was so jumpy today. Claire frowned as she recalled being told she had no sense of humour.

"I have to go and move some large muscle groups right now," she said.

"Wait, wait," he said. "You do microsurgery."

"How do you know?"

"You're trying to show how acupuncture works."

Claire said nothing.

"I know the paradigm," he said. "What's demanded. It's not always fair."

21

"You're interested in microsurgery, in acu-puncture?" She didn't stop him when he started to walk beside her.

Claire not only let him walk with her, she let him come up to the track and wait, though he hadn't insisted, or hadn't quite insisted. He agreed to stand in the corner, and there he was, tall, patient, verging on but not quite pathetic as he shifted from foot to foot and looked around.

While circuit training, Claire conspicuously talked to all the men she knew, all the fanatics that met at Hart House every lunch hour, includ-ing Daryl. She was the only woman. Music from the aerobics class below floated up.

At the chinning bar she told Daryl, "He wants to visit the animal care facility."

"I'm finished." Daryl bent over to catch his breath.

"I don't even know the guy," Claire felt com-pelled to explain. "But he knows who you are."

"Another one." Daryl straightened up and ran a big, caressing hand over his abdominal muscles. No matter what he said she knew he enjoyed being recognized, and she resented the public way he made a show of giving her a hearing, pausing to cock his head toward her. His fingers probed each indentation on his stomach; that's what really interested him.

"I don't know the guy," Claire said again.

He nodded and kept on stroking his stomach, attentive and condescending at the same time. He was attracted to her. She hated him a little even as she exercised control and made him listen. It wasn't real power, she thought.

"I'll talk to him," he said abruptly, making it clear he could have just walked away.

Introducing Daryl as chairman of biology, she watched Malcolm appear not to notice the title. He rubbed his hands together — washing them, eager to get on to what interested him.

Daryl wouldn't let him, benignly held him up with a distracted turning away. Malcolm was forced to take account of Daryl's physical presence. Nearly fifty, still running the mile in close to five minutes, Daryl made it clear in the way he stood that he had lifted weights for nearly thirty years. His long, simian arms, ending in big curved hands, hung loosely. The quadriceps of his right leg contracted, straining against his tight shorts. Long before jogging Daryl had been a runner, long before fitness classes he had been obsessed. He was a charter member of a group where sets of sit-ups could reach a thousand: dentists, deputy ministers, chiropractors, PhDs, a disproportionate number with speech impediments.

Moving aside, Claire too had to take into account Daryl's body. She saw how much shorter he was than Malcolm, that's why he'd stepped away. Malcolm had to lean forward, to stoop. And Daryl's head was too big, Claire thought, his soft grey hair, untouched by sweat, puffed out around his bald spot. He was wasp-waisted, and so tanned. Suddenly Claire knew, she just knew, that if Malcolm took off his shirt he would have undefined muscles, a straight, smooth body, the pink and white and flushed skin of the redhead. And she knew that for all his humid messiness, the wet wool of his coat, Malcolm was immaculately clean.

"You want to see rats," Daryl stated.

"Not just rats."

"You want to check out the condition of our rats," Daryl emphasized.

"I'm serious about this. I really would like a chance to get into the lab, to actually see where the research animals are kept."

"Why?"

"I'm doing an article…I'm curious. I want to know the truth. No," he said, trying to be completely honest. "I just want to see it. It's impossible to get in."

"No it isn't," Daryl said.

"Well…"

"There's no problem with access," Daryl said matter-of-factly. "But we have to be careful."

"Can I have a look, then? I have an open mind."

"There *is* a real question of security. Animal-rights zealots get in there and years of research go up in flames. And I mean flames. They'd kill the research animals to save them."

"No, they wouldn't."

"Please." The dismissal was absolute.

Claire interjected. "You need a card to get in." She was waiting for Daryl to turn on his heels.

"Open it up if there's nothing to hide." Malcolm gave an exasperated, aggressive smirk.

Daryl smiled back the same way. The look was one that was designed to pull, not rank, but a deeper memory of control, an appeal to shame in the person who dared to question. What she called parenthood. She'd seen it in politicians, the ones in power. Daryl was good at it — "I'm your father, how dare you" went along with "All right, you want to challenge me then, you want to fight." It was truly angry, it was effective, it made you scared. It could also make you fight back; it was all mixed up.

"Interference with even *one* specimen could influence research," Daryl said. "Careers are at stake, data."

"One data point doth not a theory make." Malcolm tried to be friendly again.

"We have to be careful," Daryl said with finality.

Malcolm nodded.

"You'd need a card," Daryl relented. "Clearance."

"I'm hoping you'll give me that," Malcolm said. "Hey, I won't touch anything."

Claire was surprised that Daryl lingered. He just stood there.

"No petting," Malcolm said.

Pathetic, Claire thought, but not quite. There was still a small challenge in the way Malcolm spoke, and he looked so much taller than Daryl.

"Write me." Daryl spun away.

"Is there any chance?" Malcolm asked Claire. "I know about the writing, the procedures, about how long it would take. That's why I came to you."

"He could get you in" — she tossed her hair — "if he wanted to."

"Can you?"

"Nope," she said. "But I don't see why you can't come and see where I work."

"Great."

Claire wasn't sure if there was false charm in

the hundred-watt smile Malcolm gave her, but she had not felt manipulated, or manoeuvred, into making the invitation. She wasn't sure why she had, but it had to do with Daryl as well. "Wait for me," she said.

As she was changing, Claire found herself taking extra time with her makeup. Obsessed with getting it just right, she was suddenly irritated by Malcolm. There was an ungainliness about him; he didn't have the look, the edge, she liked. Telling herself she always took time with her makeup — she even worked out in it — she decided that her lips weren't full enough.

They walked back in the rain and Claire remembered this stretch of walk in September, when she'd come back from the medical conference in Italy. She was tanned, wearing the sandals she'd bought in Milan. Toronto was bright and cool and she'd shivered. The clear sky at that time of year lied, gave her a headache. Worse was to come: the present was empty. She hated this climate.

At the lab her impatience continued. "I'll make

coffee," she said. "It's all I'm having for lunch." The blame in her voice was directed at him.

"Thanks for letting me come up." Malcolm went right over to the big easy chair under the window, the one she'd brought from home. He sat down and stretched out his long legs, oblivious to her irritation.

"Make yourself at home," she said.

"Oh, sorry." He got up.

"What do you take in your coffee?"

"Nothing," he said, then added, "It really should be open."

"The facility? It is open. You're going to drink Colombian coffee in it."

"No, I mean downstairs. That's where most of the animals are, isn't it?"

"You have to show that card."

Malcolm grimaced and scratched his head.

"There's real security there." She gave him a pottery cup. "What do you want me to do about it?"

"But nothing's happened here," Malcolm said.

"You don't know that. People have tried."

"It's like taking knowledge and locking it up in a library. Not letting anybody in."

"Library?" She paused. "People are paranoid about their research."

"Is it that, or what's going on?" he asked.

"Boy," Claire said. "Wow."

Putting the coffee down, and opening his hands like wings, letting the arguments go, Malcolm asked, "Can I see what you do?"

"Sure," she said. "It's at the end of the table."

"Right here?"

"Right here."

"I didn't notice when we came in. I haven't been in a lab like this one. It's so ordinary. But I guess it was in offices like this they decoded the double helix."

"I don't know," she said. "Take a look."

At the end of Claire's combination table and desk was a tin structure, the same shape and size as the canopy over the grill in an open kitchen, but in one corner of this fume collector was a yellow decal warning of radioactivity. Beneath the structure, stretched between two poles, little trapezes that held him underneath his haunches at one end and by his teeth at the other, was one of the things that Malcolm had failed to notice: a white rat. The weight of the animal's body hung by the hooked rodent incisors, bare and dark yellow. Claire sipped her coffee.

"This is where you work, eh?" Malcolm said.

"For hours and hours."

The rat's back, its spine, was laid open, the incision narrow and held with tiny clamps at each end. What looked like microwave wrap covered the slit. The lips of the wound were thin, fresh, bright red, contrasting with the white fur. The rodent was utterly immobile without being trussed, supported by its bare teeth.

"Jeeze," Malcolm said.

"It's anaesthetized," Claire said, then tried to laugh. "It's even on an anti-anxiety drug, BuSpar, which attenuates punishment-suppressed behaviour in animals and exerts a taming effect."

"What the hell's that mean?"

"It doesn't feel a thing. BuSpar's for people too. Want some? It's like Prozac, only doesn't stay in the system. Buspirone hydrochloride."

"It looks pretty skinny," Malcolm said. "Is that because of the way it's laid out?"

"People used to be convinced cells in the spinal cord could not reproduce nerve cells," Claire flared. "Well they can. And doing experiments on cells in petri dishes is not the same as doing it on a live animal."

"Is this animal alive?"

"Of course it's alive."

Malcolm shook his head.

"What you need is a tour of the Sick Children's Hospital," she said. "Not downstairs."

"No," he said, "I'm —"

"And there's other applications. Acupuncture."

"Do you believe in that?"

"Yes," she said. "Alternative medicine does work. It's tricky to document, but it does."

"There isn't any nature left in China."

Ignoring what he said, another invitation to argument, another red herring that felt softly, vaguely racist, Claire said, "It's not all simple. It's complicated. Look, I have to get to work."

"It's thin." To study the rat, but without

moving any closer, Malcolm tilted his head forward, giving himself a double chin. "What'd you say was wrong with it?"

"Nothing," she said. "There's nothing wrong with it. And it's thin because it's difficult to operate through ugly fat."

Turning away, Malcolm exhaled. "It's starving."

III

A Journey to the Northern Ocean

The light and mist, the ambiguity of damp mild weather, made the evening seem slack and out of joint. Daryl went down the front steps of his house, stopped and rested his hand on the wall. Uneasy, with a strange, unnatural energy for this time of day, he absent-mindedly ran his hand over the porous sandstone. He found himself thinking about Claire.

Vividly, Daryl recalled a conversation they'd had that afternoon, Claire somehow resplendent under fluorescent lights; red lipstick and a red vest so alive against her black hair and the pastel cinderblock of the corridor. As she spoke Claire laid a hand on his forearm to show she was sincere, touched him, something she'd never done before.

"It sounds strange but makes a kind of sense," she said. "A trip close to the Arctic Circle. We'll need someone like you. Why don't you come?"

Unexpected enthusiasm for what she said had surged in Daryl. For a moment he imagined freedom, forgetting even the woman in front of him.

And there was a suppressed excitement in the way Claire spoke; she addressed a world away from the biology building. Never had she approached him that way, especially him. For two years Claire had turned aside: from his jokes, from invitations to work out, from the familiar way he said hello; the way he'd first spoken to her when she walked into the lab.

When she came up to him like that Daryl had

responded by saying "Claire!", using her name as if for the first time, as if they'd just met. It must have sounded the same as before, he thought: too enthusiastic, an inappropriate friendliness that put her off. Still, he tilted his big head and tried a twisted, sheepish grin. "In a way I thought you didn't trust me."

"You're my boss."

"Then why ask *me* to go?"

"I know you. You're in good shape." She laughed. "Don't you want to see the animals?"

"Know me?"

"You're a biologist."

"Nearly nuclear," he said. "The rat man."

"It would be good to have someone familiar along, who could do it. And these things are hard to organize."

"But this guy Malcolm's putting it together?" The statement became an aggressive question, he couldn't help himself.

"One of the few untouched places left," she said.

"Nothing's untouched."

37

"Raw wilderness. Incredible wildlife."

"How do you know?"

"I'll show you where we're going," she said. "It could be special, an adventure."

"Adventure is a word that too often goes along with bad planning and disaster."

"Okay, resist," she said. "But think about it. The trip of a lifetime."

All Daryl's assumptions about Claire were called into question. He'd categorized her as defensively oblivious; slow on the uptake for sure. Some of this was resentment for the way she didn't pay attention to him, but she did seem out of it. Now he felt avid.

His hand left the wall and Daryl smoothed his shirt front, reaching down to touch his belt buckle. The bumps and indentations of his abs were deeply reassuring. Maybe he was getting down fine, a little thin. Impossible at forty-seven. His big hand left the soft cloth reluctantly.

Was this excitement about Claire or, strangely, the trip?

For a moment the petty highs and lows of

daily life didn't attach to him in light of the possibility of a journey, not so much being with Claire as a vision of mackerel clouds, a rolling, empty landscape; a place he had never been but that he saw now, clear in its silences.

The reverie left as quickly as it had come. He was overcome with resentment of Malcolm. The jerk had just demanded to see the lab, and all that he said was full of implications: about the subjects of experiments, about Daryl's character. How Daryl resented thinking up responses for Malcolm, responses to questions that hadn't even been asked! He couldn't help but do it. If Malcolm could see him with Rosie, and see how much he cared for the dog. The kids loved her. A good animal; not some scabrous mongrel from a pound that the university paid an exorbitant price for, then dewormed, inoculated, washed, fed; rescued from extinction, gave more time to, gave life itself to — and then the dog gave life to people. Often the dogs were diseased, hours from death when they were purchased. Hell, rescued.

Now he was angry in the odd, damp night. He couldn't seem to catch himself, who he was. There was something in this unnatural air of spring; he felt disembodied. The anger dissipated as quickly and inexplicably as it had come and Daryl was suddenly restless. It was the idea of a trip — if it could make routine obsessions disappear so easily, there was something to it. He was exultant.

Daryl walked and walked that evening, at least two miles down to Queen Street where the fog was dense. The humidity off the lake had the smell in it of sewage, but its yellow cast around the streetlamps was pleasant, and made the world seem reassuringly empty. He was conscious of noticing the glow, as in a picture.

The moisture in the air made him uncomfortably hot. Sweating, he took off the mackinaw jacket he had put on over his dress shirt before leaving the house.

The evening seemed so strange, not attached

to him, full of an expectant, spring-like feeling from twenty, thirty years ago. He felt, not so much transformed, but eager again.

He was alone, but his children were at home, asleep in the room next to his. Before going out he had stood at their door and listened to their breathing.

Thoughts of his children made him recall the child in the face of Laura, whom he had driven home earlier, the windows of the car wet and clouding, the defog fan roaring ineffectively.

At one point he responded to something she said, he couldn't even remember what, by saying, "Don't be stupid," turning the steering wheel with one hand, speaking harshly simply because he was frustrated. The day had been long and difficult.

It was as if he'd struck her. Instantly, in a moment of charged sexuality, she'd hung her head, opened her mouth, and murmured, "Sorry."

She'd done so much work for him — he almost thought of her as a research assistant and not a librarian — and this was how he acted. Her head actually dropped forward and her neck curved as she stared at the dashboard.

"Sorry," she murmured again, breathing through her mouth, her lips parted. Laura, who lived with her cats, short brown hair with grey threads in it, pale skin and a husky, nearly expressionless voice that seemed to match her eyes; her profile that of a punished child's.

What had he conjured up? He had spoken brutally because he was able to, and Laura would not hit back. But this sexuality, this bass note — bowel music was how he thought of it later — was so strong. There was confusion; in his head the buzzing of insects, the stone cry of the locust.

"Sorry," she'd breathed again.

"Hey, come on," he made himself say. "There's nothing to be sorry about," thinking no one should ever take advantage of a child this way. "Hey," he said loudly, as if to wake them both up.

"Sorry," she repeated, and Daryl was afraid; afraid of the depth of her response, afraid of her passion. Any self-congratulating morality he may have felt was also an act of self-preservation. Conscience was a way of extricating himself.

He would go to the Arctic. There was a place of simple biology, beyond the treeline; in one day he'd be able to name all the species.

A furnace fear rushed out as soon as he made the decision, panic about leaving his family, the familiar, and he did not trust Malcolm. But he would go. It wasn't that long a trip, Claire would be there, the pilots would know where they were.

In mist and rain, in the middle of a city, Daryl thought of Laura, of Claire, of his children. He imagined a cold wind on his face; this night's darkness, but with winter's edge in it. And he imagined sunlit plains, tundra before it turned green, the coming of summer.

Daryl started to make plans and compile lists, not of what he would need, but of arguments he would make to Malcolm. Science, he ran it over and over, *is* nature. Science is the truth about nature, a way of seeing what is really there. Scientific medicine does not reject or distort nature but achieves its results by recognizing what nature is and reproducing and reconstituting her grand designs. There are some sacrifices, there is a price to pay, but science is not a blasphemy; wilful rejection of its insights is. Oh, he would have fun. He turned for home.

IV

The Birds of the Air

There were ravens on the water tower and it never got dark. The night was the worst, ever. One-thirty a.m., Pelican Narrows Motel, curtains closed to keep out a sky that had a huge glow inside it, the glow of morning monstrous and unhealthy, luminous, a light that would never go away.

There was no night, this wasn't twilight, just restlessness, headachy dawn, no rest: sheets atwist, looking yellow in the glow of the bedside lamp. They felt damp though she wasn't sweating. Too many showers, and she didn't, couldn't concentrate on drying off properly.

The room was too hot, too cold; she got up, lay down, took another shower, turned on the TV, turned it off: the emotion seemed greater than anything she'd experienced before.

Panic.

The word was meaningless, had nothing to do with what she was feeling, the most intense feelings of her life. The worst, the worst.

Unable to sleep, unable to pace, she paced. Not wanting to take another half Valium, to use them all up, no more to be had, they were leaving tomorrow, she took one: no help. Frantic.

Unable to sit, unable to read; standing up, lying down; she was going to explode. It couldn't get worse and did.

It did. The panic, the terror, kept coming. Those words didn't describe it. The only thing clear was it came in waves, always in waves, that was what she was most sure about. Each flood seemed the same as the one before, not stronger, not weaker, unbearable. Each one was stronger, and she bore it. So strong, stronger than anything.

And she saw it all happening, saw herself sitting at the edge of the bed in T-shirt and underpants, objectively looking down at herself as if her spirit or something, some part of her mind, was on the ceiling. She watched herself get up and go wash her hands again. The bathroom was damp, dim. There was water on the floor. She unwrapped another tiny soap, the last one. Her hands shook.

Waves. Waiting for the next one.

Before, fear had been so various. Such variety had fear: it could change temperature and colour, taste and odour, hit her high or low. Sensations of an indeterminate nature so often resolved themselves into fear. The snotty, weeping child within, the little girl that needed to be mothered, fathered, taken care of. The contemporary

God. Utter crap now. This *was* new. Looking at her forearm, the bone of her forearm, the hand that held the soap, she saw her tan yellow, jaundiced in the light. Her whole body felt loose-jointed, bony, skeletal. Skin, small flesh soft on bone. Flabby.

She would never get over this, never get her body back, never sleep, never be hungry again.

Walking to the motel door, opening it. The enormous grey sky, tinged with orange-pink, seemed to churn with intensity, yet the clouds didn't move. Down the road huskies howled. They were chained beside dog houses, chained up all season, beside the oiled dirt road that led to the airport, to the airplane that would take them away in a few hours. Malcolm had wanted to let the dogs loose. He had no plan, it wasn't his business, he just wanted to let them go. The fool.

To have allowed someone like him to persuade her to come to a place like this. One moment of stupid enthusiasm for a big change, a different world: an impulse that led to Fort Smith, where nothing good could ever start.

She stepped outside. Though it was cold the air was humid, hard to breathe. Goose bumps rose on her legs. Cement from the sidewalk was harsh on the bottom of her feet. She shivered and went back inside.

That wave subsided. She could think a little.

There was no connection with Malcolm, he was not a lover, or a friend, and yet he had got her here.

Last night, after the absurd meeting about hiring the boy to help out, they had gone for a walk, down to the Rapids of the Drowned. He said all the things he'd said before about the trip, but her trance had begun; she heard him but it was meaningless. She was feeling the place, what it was to her. It struck Claire that Malcolm's hymn to the Far North had been meaningless the first time — yet she'd come. Given up three weeks of summer to come here. And she knew, tomorrow, she would fly in. It could not be stopped.

The mosquitoes had been intolerable; the insect repellent oily and irritating. Spruce pressed in, the path led down, the roar came closer. She was nothing in it.

"Can you believe you're here," Malcolm had said. There was suppressed excitement in his voice that she resented.

With a wave of nausea she wondered what she'd do for three weeks in his company, in a place she'd never been.

"So what does it look like?" she said.

"The tundra or the Slave?" he asked, being deliberately obtuse, pushing aside willows and alders.

"Don't be stupid," she said. Though Malcolm was sweating, the hair lying across his skull looked dry, reminding her of the red hair she'd seen on the picture of an exhumed corpse, a Guatemalan victim videotaped in the brightest colour. Preserved.

"It's beautiful," he said. "Green rolling tundra, the arctic prairies, and you can see all around. When I first canoed the Thelon I expected the worst, but then I thought, hey, this is easy. I can show this to other people."

He was not trying to reassure her, as he had before. The time she asked about rapids he'd joked, "We'll bring you back alive," and what he said worked because he was so consciously making an effort, and there was that warmth in his voice. Now he seemed to be just reporting. Which made her angry. She let the word *easy* slip by, meaningless, and focused on how quickly her moods could change. Before them she was a sleepwalker, hollow and helpless.

"I want to go back," she said.

"What?"

Claire kept moving, going down, not smelling the damp spruce that pressed in on them, not seeing the ground, but remembering flying in from Calgary and having the same sick fear she had now as the plane lurched and dropped with turbulence. Then the smooth approach to Fort Smith, seeing it from the air. An unexpected lifting of her heart, the joy of wellbeing. The appreciation she felt on seeing the place was suspect, of the same species as the panic, but so welcome. Hope was uncannily like a drug: she had never seen anything like this northern town with its tiny shining spire — the sun was out — but it was like a memory. This was what she had wanted, she felt, this is why she had come. The North, the river, the thing itself.

On the trail Claire tried to hold on to how moved she had been, and she tried to understand it. Was the scene expected, familiar from old magazines, those copies of the *Beaver* her father subscribed to? Joe Boyer, worked at the refinery all his life, but dreamed. Kept silent, and drove down to the St. Clair River, under the bridge, to imagine the Great Lakes. He'd never sailed away, and now he was dead.

She missed her father so much now she was weepy. He would never have imagined travelling so far, but he would have lit up when told of it. Were his desires why she had recognized Fort Smith? But guessing at the source of her feelings, even understanding them, did not help. When had it ever? And in her acknowledgement of Fort Smith there was something greater: large, huge, everlasting.

"How many people will ever get to see what we will see," Malcolm said, "will ever go on a trip like this? The great herds of the African savanna are just remnants. There's nothing left anywhere in the world. But the tundra still has large numbers of animals, caribou. A river of life."

He was right, but she was afraid again, and they emerged into a tumult of water and pelicans and the immense Slave. But there was no bright light. She trembled, wasn't interested in the pelicans, and she knew, she just knew that she could never live in Fort Smith. Life was meaningless, there was no frame, unless you were in a city. Only there could you get up in the morning and have it mean anything; even with comfortable despair something might happen. Here all you would ever do is feel you were missing something.

This was a place you could only look back on.

"Does that friend of yours…"

"Big Bill," Malcolm said.

"Big Bill. Does his wife teach school?"

"Yep."

"I thought so. I almost heard him say school teacher lady. He's ridiculous."

"I know. But he's also a good guy. He knows a lot. And his kid will help us. He's a good kid."

"Really." She was afraid again. It was uncanny, as if she was condemned, had taken a job here, had signed a year-long contract and now wanted to quit. How would she face winter? All that time, passing, passing her by.

"Jeeze, the bugs are bad," Malcolm said. "Do you want to go back?"

"What's it like?" she said distractedly.

"I told you. But you'll see tomorrow. It's not like the bush. You can see all around. The lichen's different colours. It's country."

"Country," she said. "That's a romantic word. Like *land*."

"It has an honourable history. It's an honourable concept."

"Jesus," she said. Then, "How did you get to know him?"

"Big Bill?"

Claire slapped her neck, then looked at her hand. There was blood on her fingers.

"Through hunting," he said.

"Hunting!" She was cold.

"I grew up with it. So did Bill. Don't be surprised. People wake up."

"Hunting," she said again.

"I wrote for a hunting magazine, and I came up here and met Bill."

"And you worry about animals in labs, chained-up dogs."

"The best game wardens are former poachers," he said.

"Right," she said.

"My father hunted and was probably one of the best bird-watchers in North America."

She did not answer him.

"I know," he said with such neutral intimacy she was taken aback, as if he did know how she felt, was sympathetic and was revealing himself at the same time, making himself vulnerable. "It's contradictory, I know."

She still did not say anything.

"I lived for it when I was a kid," he went on. "Lived for it. I couldn't get enough fall. I loved the fall." Malcolm waited a moment, giving Claire a chance to respond.

"We lived near Pickering," he said. "It wasn't like now. It's ruined now. Maybe there can never be any more hunting."

"This obsession with animals."

"I came up here to study wolves, to see their impact on the caribou herd," he said.

"Yes," she said bitterly. "Wolves are competitors for hunters."

"Right," he admitted. "And Big Bill was a wolf hunter, or he pretended to be. Look at the size of those birds."

She was not interested in pelicans.

"And I realized that anyone who would shoot a wolf would shoot a man," Malcolm said.

"A wolf is the same as a person," she said with flat challenge.

"Anyway, Big Bill made himself out to be — he was hustling. I don't think he'd even seen a wolf. He was trying to make a living."

"And you trust him to help us."

"He's a great guy," Malcolm said. "Really. He does know a tremendous amount about this country. And I need his son."

"His wife supports him," she said.

"We're hiring Billy," Malcolm said. "There's experience there. And Billy's young. Energy. Make it easier."

She couldn't concentrate. Malcolm kept talking.

"The guy really does have a feel for the place. He likes the peace and quiet."

"Who?"

"Big Bill."

Peace and quiet was a synonym for all the depression and terror in the world, she thought. A disquieting wave; a howling emptiness. She felt she could not bear peace and quiet.

"I felt I couldn't say anything to him about his river," Malcolm explained.

He keeps on about Big Bill, she thought, as if being stubborn about him would persuade her.

"He loves it," Malcolm said. "And he loves

poplars. Others call them weed trees. Bill loves the deep poplar green. Well, you won't believe how glad we'll be to see any trees at all when we get back. This place will seem like a jungle, like a rainforest."

That is what they had talked about at the wide river. She had barely glanced at it, recoiling from the mud and the sound. And they had stopped talking as they toiled back up into town. Just once Malcolm pointed out a spruce that he said Big Bill had hugged when he first came to Fort Smith. The big tree was part of some private moment that had persuaded him to settle there, and was still the same after ten years, unchanged. Claire half heard the anecdote, and then they emerged into the open spaces of the town out of breath, avoiding where the bank of the river had caved in. Cloud came in and covered the sun that never set, what wind there was faded, and the air became still and oily. Insects tormented them, tiny mosquitoes, tiny stings that didn't abate, even on the open streets. Little black dots, specks of soot, which hurt. Back to the room to try to sleep, and all that went along with that futile exercise. It must be early morning now. She refused to look at the clock; she had to get some sleep.

But she didn't even lie down. Claire turned the TV on, pulled back the curtains. Evangelical television was going, had gone on through the night.

Sun came out now, it was three-thirty a.m., sun through the massive clouds, and she heard "washed in the blood of the lamb" from the television. She heard, "See, see, how Christ's blood streams in the firmament." Claire shivered. The hair stood on the back of her neck. She must have been shivering from shock, she felt, from lack of sleep, yet suddenly how bright was the world, how sunny, how vaulted the sky: truly all glory. And on the broken stone of the motel's parking lot, on rusted railing and cement, was dew. The engines of night, the towering clouds — cauldrons of rose and banked fire — were replaced: by the clearest morning of all the world. They were leaving soon, on the long flight in. Missing a night's sleep would make no difference. All was fresh washed, but not in blood. God was this clarity.

V

The Dismal Lakes, the September Mountains

"This seat's been broken," Billy said quietly as he guided one of the canoes ashore.

"What?" Malcolm bounded over, making a splash.

"Take it easy," said the pilot. "That can't be."

Malcolm bent over the canoe, then turned a round face upward: "Well, it is."

"Wait a minute," the pilot asserted.

"You've got to be careful how you lash them!"

"Let's see." Daryl joined them, moving with excessive calm.

Tipping back his Stetson, Billy stood aside. Both Daryl and Malcolm leaned into the boat and the pilot jumped down off the float of the airplane.

"I don't know how it could happen," the pilot said. "It's a new canoe."

"You have to use the thwarts," Malcolm said. "Seats aren't strong enough."

"Yeah, well…"

"We can prop this up," Daryl said, "and tie it on. Do you have any wire?" he asked the pilot.

"I don't know."

"So you're going to be a prick about it!" Malcolm exploded.

"Hey…"

"Take it easy," Daryl spoke in a rich, slow, self-satisfied voice. Yet there was an irritated quaver in it. "He might not pick us up if you piss him off."

"No, I, hey…," the pilot said.

Malcolm pushed on the seat. "I should have kept an eye on you guys."

"Don't break it." Daryl spoke sharply now.

"I normally use the thwarts." The pilot stared at the sheared bolt and hanging seat.

So their first hours on the tundra would be spent with the men huddled over the canoe the way they would huddle over a car engine, Claire thought, giving advice and competing to see who could show the most ingenuity fixing it.

Coarse sand crunched under her feet; one of her boots had been soaked when she jumped to shore. Cranberries, withered and so deeply red they were almost purple, clung to the bank. There was a mat of lichen and bearberry.

Across open water, she saw a frozen bay. Clouds clung like snowsqualls to a land of low relief.

On landing, Claire had felt surprise, acutely aware of what she thought of as very fresh air. It was quiet. Yet even with the engine of the plane shut off she continued to inhabit a loud place. Turmoil, reverberation: her mind. She still had to go to the bathroom and went inland to find some bushes.

Flying in, she'd been strangely numb. At Fort Smith there had been no overcast. In very, very early morning — farther south it would have been dark — she'd found Daryl and Billy waiting for her by the side of the motel. The men squatted on their haunches and rested their backs against the wall as they also waited for Billy's father. Big Bill was going to drive them and their gear to the float plane base. Malcolm was already out there.

The symphony of night fears abated a little as she said hello and looked at them, so prepared in their clean socks with the pants tucked into the tops — as expectant and vulnerable as she. The sun and its flood of light was red, sore looking, but the parking lot and its fringe of grass so wet and sparkling it seemed everything might turn out all right.

As she'd sat crunched in the cold of the airplane her panic came back. But it was muted. She had to pee — it was all too late now. Quickly, just over the huge Slave River, they'd flown into cloud. All Claire had to do to step out into space was press on what looked like the handle of an old car. Drops of rain on the cabin windows, a sour taste, brought a memory of childhood despair that made her sleepy. She was between resignation, boredom, and terror. In the seat beside her Daryl's head dropped forward and he shut his eyes; he was making himself unconscious.

What she could see of land, intermittently, was sere, rust coloured. There were black puddles; they must be ponds.

The clouds had parted, or else they'd flown under them, and she'd seen lakes, big lakes, below. Covered in ice, they seemed to be significant, and the pilot turned to her and gestured downward, pantomiming the words "Lynx Lake" above the vibrating, high-pitched roar.

What looked like snowmobile tracks — they couldn't be — crossed the ice far below. If only they were snowmobile tracks; there might be some help for them.

Near the edges of the snowy ice was a border of aquamarine; a long fissure ran down the centre. The anomalous tropical colour reminded her of gloomy March in Sarnia, of slush flowing in the St. Clair River. A similar patch of aquamarine waited, nearly out of sight, on the horizon of Lake Huron.

Going down, brown spots on the tundra had turned, wheeled, and fled from the plane. They were so small.

The pitch of the engine changed. Claire leaned forward to enquire about the dots — they looked like grouse, like something she'd never seen. Their mute cohesion was insect-like and shocked her.

"Musk ox," mouthed the pilot. He was excited.

The brown spots wheeled again. What was loose in their motion must have been fur.

There was another small group, this time of grey dots, that also wheeled and turned together in the same way, but more quickly.

"Caribou." The pilot shook his head in disbelief. So many animals.

Claire didn't know what she had expected, but it was nothing like this. She was aware she was in a plane, high up, but seeing wildlife so instantly made her realize that there had been an abstraction in her whole idea of them: now they were here she couldn't quite believe in them. Their singleness of purpose was alien, an affront.

The bare rounded hills were coming up fast and she lost sight of the turning herds.

On the ground there was nothing. No trace of musk ox or caribou. Now, as the airplane taxied out, the men stood to watch; they seemed grateful that their squabbling gave them a distraction and they could avoid being solemn about the plane leaving. Its roar was eaten quickly and the wind began to blow.

There were no trees, but Claire found some willows for a screen even though she was out of sight of the beach. After buttoning her slacks back up she decided to stay where she was for a moment, leaving the organizing to the others.

There was some life nearby. On a pond, just behind her, a single oldsquaw sat motionless, its tail feather outlined like a needle against the surface of the water.

She supposed that seeing it helped.

"Jesus, it's about forty degrees."

"It's colder than that."

"It's really dropped."

At Billy's suggestion they had turned a canoe over to form a windbreak. It didn't help much, as the wind kept changing direction. All of them stood. Malcolm broke a willow switch and poked at a pot heating on a propane stove. It was taking a long time to boil.

"Man, that wind just sucks the heat away," he said and lifted the lid.

"Well, don't let it out," Daryl said. "Jeeze, that'll cost you more BTUs."

There was nowhere to hide; the tundra was wet, and fine rain came and went and felt like spindrift, like needles, like sand.

"When we get farther south there'll be wood," Malcolm said. "We can have fires at night."

"There won't be any night," Billy said.

"That's good." Claire huddled more deeply into her ski jacket, arms crossed and hugging her chest. "Somehow that's good."

Daryl was studying a topographic map, protected in a plastic case. "I thought the best thing to do was to start south and meet the summer," he said.

"I don't know why you're bringing the route up now," Claire said to him. "We talked about it enough before." She wondered if she should go and get a rain jacket to put over her coat.

"It's what a lot of parties do," Billy said, though he hadn't thought about it, and didn't look at anyone as he spoke; he didn't even seem to be agreeing with Daryl.

"Well." Malcolm paused. "We'll go up this lake and across the height of land, then down the unnamed river. As we discussed. Then we'll meet up with the Thelon, where the Hornby party once came in. And we could run into the big migration. *Idthen!*"

"What?" Daryl snapped.

"Caribou," Billy said. "And Hornby didn't run into the migration."

"And died because of it," Malcolm said. "But we're here for different reasons."

"Who was Hornby?" Claire asked.

"One of the first to come up with the idea for the game sanctuary," Billy said. "He starved to death on the Thelon with his nephew and another guy in the twenties."

"And the Thelon'll be easy," Daryl stated.

Billy shrugged and said, "Hornby was kind of a nut. His nephew left a diary about that winter. In a way Hornby killed his companions. He took a lot of chances."

"But he had the bug," Malcolm said. "He looked at this place differently than people did back then."

"What bug?" said Billy. "He cut things too close."

"He didn't run around like most of the natives and trash the joint," Malcolm said.

"The natives didn't trash the joint."

"I meant the white trappers, the silver fox

trappers, back then," Malcolm said. "Hornby had the spirit."

"So now what?" Claire asked.

"Now what." Daryl's mockery had general anger in it, though he addressed Claire. "Why, this is it. We're here."

"But what do we do now?"

"Eat, get warm," said Billy. "Stay dry. Get into the tent."

"Unaccommodated man," Malcolm said. "A poor, bare, forked animal." Before anyone could answer, he looked at Billy and spoke confidingly. "Could you believe it, coming in. So many animals."

"It wasn't up close," Billy said. "But I'm going to count it. There were more than I've seen in my life. And all at once!"

"They're around," Daryl joined in.

Everyone's mood improved. Malcolm put packets of freeze-dried food into the pot and said, "Well, even if we don't see anything else we can die happy."

"That's it. I've had it," Daryl said. "Why are you always saying things like that?"

"I don't know what you mean."

"Dropping bombs like that."

It was awfully early for this kind of thing to develop, Billy thought, taking his hat off and examining it, stepping back from the canoe. Claire sunk deeper into her coat. The wind seemed louder.

"Look, look!" Malcolm pointed across the bay. "Look at that."

A wolf, small because of the distance, yet the edges of its white fur looking matted, touched with yellow, trotted across open ground.

"Look at that," Daryl said wonderingly.

"How many people live all their lives in the bush and never see a wolf?" Billy's question was to no one in particular.

"Why is its fur like that?" Claire asked. "It's blurry." And then she said, "I've never seen anything move that way in my life."

"Maybe it doesn't see us," Billy said.

"It's aware," Daryl said. "It has to be."

"We'll go over tomorrow and have a look." Malcolm, tall and immobile, slowly lifted the arm holding his cooking stick. "There'll be a den nearby." He pointed.

"You think so?" Daryl said.

"It's the time of year."

The light in the tent was unnatural. It was so late, and so bright. The blue nylon walls flapped and beat, the frame shook. No rain was getting through but there seemed to be a fine mist inside. Claire was surprisingly warm in her sleeping bag, zipped up with just her eyes, nose, and cheeks out; her nose must have been red. As she tried to curl up she panicked briefly, thinking she felt damp, but it was only a cold spot. A metallic smell was in the air, and she wondered if it was her polypropylene underwear getting sour already, or the nylon sleeping bag cover, or just the cold. She might have to tie a kerchief over her eyes to get to sleep.

A shadow passed beside the wall of her tent, then settled at the door. She thought of a cloud, but the sky was a uniform canopy out there, a glowing grey midnight sky; yet darkness was collected and it spoke.

"Claire?"

Malcolm.

"I'm sleeping."

"Okay, but the pilot mentioned we might have to stay here a couple of days."

"Why are you telling me now? Tell me in the morning."

"Do you think we should move?"

"We'll talk in the morning. We'll just be sensible about it." For godsakes, she thought.

"I know that. We'll bring you back alive." He chortled, saying what he'd said before but with such unambiguous goodwill and sincerity Claire warmed to him. She felt giddy. "We're not going to charge down anything," Malcolm said. "We'll look. I can't believe it's one of those rivers you charge down."

And suddenly she was very happy.

"Can you believe you're here?" Malcolm repeated. He didn't want to go away.

"Yes," she said, going deeper into her bag. It was all there was.

VI

"...But How Can One Be Warm Alone?"

When she was naked she arranged her clothes,
her sleeping bag, her books and diary in a circle.
Protected in this nest she let the sun warm her.
Just inches above the tiny walls she had constructed it felt cool, but where she basked lying
on her stomach was a centre of buttery heat.
There was a little air on her legs, which raised

goose bumps, but she stretched out then relaxed, as at home with her body as she had ever been.

Who would have thought it? The place had a stark, fairyland quality. Trees so green against sand and lichen. Though the river in front of her was grey, except in the shallows where the water was transparently clear, behind her were lakes of bright blue and dark jade. The words used to explain such places — and Daryl and Malcolm were full of them: *esker, microclimate, oasis* — had no connection with the place itself. It seemed she was about to experience the true dimensions of the situation in which she had placed herself.

"Claire."

She pulled her sleeping bag over her. Couldn't she even air it without being bothered! Now brittle broken lichen attached to her stomach. Deliberately she'd camped far from the others, the wonderful weather giving her confidence; she'd stopped worrying about anything.

"We're going for a hike." They were in the woods behind her, in a depression, out of sight. "Want to come along?"

Daryl and Malcolm. There was neutrality in their voices, they didn't emerge and surprise her; she couldn't really be angry.

"No, go ahead. I've got a good spot here." Why couldn't she say she wanted to be by herself?

"Okay," they said. Were they watching? "See you later."

A good spot! Malcolm had talked of dying here, or of having his ashes flown in and scattered. That kind of talk didn't matter anymore.

She remembered the first morning in the boats, dressed in winter clothes, none of them familiar with their canoeing partners; awkward and silent and scared. What good were the life-jackets, all the bulk on their bodies, with the water temperature what it was? The ice lining the open river, its colour and layers, she remarked with a kind of paralyzed indifference. The paddle felt thick as an oar.

The day ahead was as blank as the landscape. The crystalline space made her fantasize that, if she went over a rise, she would come upon a new, but deserted, parking lot.

At least Billy, in the stern of her canoe, was competent. Daryl and Malcolm zigzagged and bickered.

But the light changed as the day went on. They'd progressed rapidly. By noon the air, as fresh as it had been in the morning, was clearer. There was happiness, and daylight daylight daylight, all the time.

Once they had got going there had been little respite in the paddling, but that didn't matter. They were getting somewhere, getting on; there was a mutual, immediate response to the country. Malcolm pointed out and commented on the shapes of islands or hills, Daryl spotted ducks or other birds, and Billy tried to imitate the cries of gulls and terns — all the hundreds of small things that made up the world about them they seemed to appreciate. Alert, they constantly searched bays and the horizons for more large mammals.

In sunshine, wading the canoes down the side of the river didn't bother them, and even if they had to portage there was no dallying or painful exploration — they could see in front of them, all around; they knew where they were going. If they rushed loads over as fast as they could it was because they were going somewhere, and then they had arrived at this place.

She slept and awoke still warm and looked out over the water. Stretching again she stood up, suddenly chilled in the light wind, and walked down to the beach, to sit on a rock with her feet in the water. Small waves broke on the sand and there were no tiny squares of organic matter, small flags of dead leaves, in the ebb and flow as there would have been down south. It was so clear and cold and her feet flushed red immediately, a bone ache, much deeper than the red flesh. Still, in the shallows, above the sand, it would be much warmer than anywhere else.

She waded out, hesitated a long time, knowing she would do it, then squatted down. Icy. She stood up. Then, in a foot and a half of water, over bright yellow sand, she threw herself in.

Her head ached, her whole body flushed, she felt wonderful. Drawing her hair back with both hands, she lifted her face to the sun.

Running back up to her things, she dried off.

The towel felt rough, the nap hard, as if it had been wet and wind-dried. Claire had an urge, almost a compulsion, to get busy, to organize, pack, unpack, get going. There was nowhere to go; she made herself stop.

Still not getting dressed, Claire walked over to the point. Malcolm had said not to put her tent there: too exposed. Sure it was a nice day, but the barometer he carried was dropping — not a place to camp.

Well, someone had camped there. In a small sandy depression were flakes and chips of stone. She bent and examined white flakes; beyond a doubt they had been chipped. Then she saw an ochre piece that had been cleanly split in half from a larger body. One side was flat, the other had a ridge from which chips had been pressed. It fitted the hand so well and had probably been used to push up, to scrape. The ball of her thumb rested on the sloped back, and the contours made her think of the body of a whale just emerged and visible above the ocean; she squeezed the spine. Thousands of miles from the ocean, but the shape was that of a whale. It fitted perfectly into her hand. She extended it in front of her, looking at it at the end of her bare arm, exposed in the wind and light.

"It would be great to have a cabin back in those lakes. Come in here some spring and wait for the caribou." Malcolm fed brittle branches of wood into the fireplace he'd constructed. "This is on the way. What a place to see them come through!"

"I've never been to a spot like this," Billy said. "I've seen the open taiga at treeline. But nothing like this."

"It's like a park," Claire said, dressed in clean clothes and dry socks, sitting with her knees drawn up to her chin.

"Worth the whole trip, really," Daryl said to her. "You should have come on the walk. We found some tent poles inland, almost preserved looking, grey. Quite old."

"Things last a long time," Billy said. "They don't deteriorate quickly out here."

Claire wasn't sure she would tell anyone about what she had found. There would be a debate: was it a camp or chipping site, Inuit or Indian? She was curious about what the implements she had found were made of. Maybe she'd ask later.

"You can't say how old those are," Billy continued. "But they are teepee poles. And the curved board that was with them looked like it could have belonged to a toboggan. They'd have come in late winter, early spring. I don't think they wintered here unless there were caribou around all winter — and there weren't. They came in from treeline."

"How do you know they didn't travel from the north?" Daryl challenged.

"I know from my dad that nobody canoed way out here. I mean they canoed, but only to ferry across rivers. They walked."

"Following the migration," Malcolm said. "Like wolves. Finding places to meet it. Fords. They did use canoes to hunt, though."

"Sure," Billy agreed.

As Billy and Malcolm spoke, Claire watched

Daryl gather himself and get ready to join in. And he glanced over at her knowingly, as if they shared common, cynical knowledge about Malcolm and Billy. She was not an ally of his! He couldn't stand to be left out, to have them know more than he. A question was coming, one with an air of honest inquiry, one that would cause an argument.

"Have you actually seen the migration?" Daryl asked, full of portentous concern, suggesting Billy had a disease.

She wanted to hit Daryl. Why had he called out to her to go for a walk when it was so obvious she'd wanted to be by herself? Hiding in the bushes.

"No," Billy said. "It's supposed to be the greatest."

"Why?"

"People just talk about it. If you ever see it you never forget it. My dad talks about it all the time."

"Has he seen it?"

"No."

"Maybe it's the energy, the aura." Malcolm poked busily at his fire. "Not measurable."

"If there's energy there'll be evidence." Daryl looked perkily at Malcolm and cocked his head.

He's refreshed, Claire thought, and if he makes fun of himself a little it's because he feels immune.

When Malcolm didn't reply at once, Daryl briefly looked confused, pursing his lips and turning his big head away. He seemed to have concentrated so hard on looking bright and ready that for a moment he wasn't sure just what he'd said or even where he was. The flesh was so tight on his bones, yet the lines at his throat, right above his T-shirt, running over the cords in his neck, were softly wrinkled, like a boy's.

Closing one eye, and still not replying, Malcolm sliced open a packet of the same dried food they'd eaten yesterday. He poured it into the pot. "Big Bill's Beans!"

"He's not here to cook them," Daryl said. "We need a cook."

"Caribou's the best meat," Billy said.

"Have you eaten caribou?" Daryl asked.

"I'd like to hunt one," Malcolm cut in. "I

mean, you couldn't stalk one and get close, but imagine spearing one, a dozen, in a caribou pound and then butchering them with a quartzite knife. Wearing the skin. Of course it took seven skins to outfit a man completely."

Quartzite. That answered her question about the objects she'd found. They were made of quartzite.

"It's a bit early to be thinking of steaks," Billy said. "We just got out here."

"You'd have to skin it out," Malcolm went on. "Undress it. Easier on a small animal like a fox but the same principle. Like taking a sweater off a child. Pull it up the arms and over the head."

"Inside out." Billy illustrated by jerking his arms upward.

"Off a child." Daryl looked at Malcolm, his eyes flat, mineral bright below heavy brows, behind axe-like cheekbones. "You know I've got kids."

In spite of the provoking things he said, Malcolm somehow reassured Claire. The way he had revealed what the chipped stone was made of without her saying a word was disconcerting, but not unexpected. He hadn't read her mind, but seemed, in so much that he did, to bump into some kind of truth. He's here for a purpose, she found herself thinking.

"I'm not going to think about skinning." Claire diverted the men, recalling at the same time incisions she had made: precise, the tiny controlled bloom, so different than tearing off a whole skin.

"We're not here for that." Malcolm smiled. His face was red — not like he had a high colour or broken veins, more a deep, permanent blush; his skin was rubbery and mobile. "You must get enough of that in the lab."

"Not really." She frowned, angry at herself for trusting him.

"Oh, please." Daryl's big hand curled and he looked down to contemplate the veins on his forearm; fat as a bowling pin above a thin wrist.

"What?" Malcolm innocently slid another piece of wood under the fire grate. The long sleeves of his tan shirt were sweat-streaked and smudged; he smelled.

"Vivisection," Daryl said. "You're going to start talking about vivisection."

"And butchery, and leather," Malcolm said. "It's complicated."

"So tell me the difference," Daryl said.

Billy turned away and faced the river, narrowing his eyes. Like Claire and Daryl he wore clean clothes, and his hair, so soft it seemed he'd just washed it, tossed a little in the breeze.

Claire tugged at the hem of her slacks, surprised they still held a crease.

"Define and discriminate?" Malcolm didn't look at Daryl.

"What's the difference between your little fantasy of death, of living off the land — a dozen caribou? — and vivisection? Life for life. One life for others' lives, many other lives."

"Living off the land isn't death," Billy spoke.

Malcolm picked at a scab on his knuckle. "It turned out to be for Hornby."

"When do *we* eat?" Claire asked.

"If people missed the caribou migration they could starve to death." Billy was matter-of-fact. "They had to be part of it."

"You're not serious." Daryl ignored Billy and looked at Malcolm. "You're just not serious."

"Serious about what?" Claire snapped.

"I can assure you I am," Malcolm said. "I am serious about death."

"Jesus," Daryl said.

Claire lifted her chin and didn't look at either of them.

"Okay," Daryl said. "Fine."

Because he thinks I'm appealing to him he looks smug, Claire thought, the way he looked at work when he knew he'd get his way and was making what he called a "tough" decision: one that wouldn't affect him.

"Want to go for a walk?" Daryl asked her. By leaning forward and showing that he couldn't get close to the fire, which Malcolm seemed to surround, he made it clear that he wasn't able to help with the cooking.

"Life for life?" Malcolm wouldn't let it go. "Maybe. But there's a difference. What I'm talking about means you have to get your shoulder in there; flesh against flesh."

Daryl had Claire's attention and did what she wanted; he did not respond.

Billy filled the silence. "What do you mean?" he asked Malcolm.

"A wolf has to bump up against the caribou it wants to kill. There are hammering hooves, at least speed. They have to engage."

"Does a wolf carry a spear?" Daryl asked as he got up. "Let alone a bow and arrow? And I could also answer you by saying" — there was a sneer in his smile — "that we engage with experimental animals on the deepest level, on the cellular level."

"The Chips thought they were wolves," Billy said. "Because they lived like them, following the deer."

"We're not Chips," Daryl said. "And we're not wolves. But I'd surely like to see some. Come on, Claire."

As they walked away Billy called after them: "The tent poles up there are Chippewayan."

On the rolling tundra, beyond where the trees

ended, the long angled light of early evening went on and on: a sunset that would last hours, with the sun never going down. It was bright, their faces were oily, and the sky itself seemed scoured, polished with wind shine.

"Those poles aren't far," Daryl said. He was irritated by the smaller depressions of land, where the groundcover would swell in hummocks and tussocks.

"Oh."

"You should have come earlier."

Had he been as petulant when he called out to her from the screen of trees earlier in the day? She was glad she had not gone. Claire tossed her hair. "It's nice out here."

"The pressure has to be climbing." Daryl stopped, closed his eyes, and raised his face to the hills.

Claire looked back down the valley. Small flames from the cooking fire were in long shadow; the tents of the men were sky blue and small, near the water. Hers could not be seen.

"Come on. We'll find the remains." Daryl

started toward rising ground so they could walk on gravel and lichen. She was glad he went quickly.

The poles were of silver, with axe marks, not tumbled or piled but still together, unmistakable evidence. She also found two pieces of wood, curved, that fit together: a toboggan.

Daryl was silent and looked at the spaced tumble on the ground. She took out her camera and photographed. What was uncanny was that where they were seemed to have never been occupied, to have never had anything to do with people. It was so empty, with only a shadow: someone stepping out of a tent in March to look at the weather. Everything else was the bright air, where they were now; so present, so fresh.

Daryl stood close as she took her pictures. She kneeled to get away from him.

"Maybe there's places people shouldn't go," Daryl said.

She looked up, surprised.

"You know I'm in a loveless marriage."

VII

Curse This Pitching

The light was inescapable, and he wasn't sure of time. Shutting his eyes didn't help. In spite of three days of overcast and low sky the luminosity inside the tent didn't change and made his head ache. There was never any darkness, only a kind of twilight.

It must be midmorning: wind-driven drizzle

crackled against the walls of the tent. He'd fall-
en asleep after breakfast and was cold. The
bottom of his sleeping bag stayed soaked even
where he'd piled a pack and waterproof bags
under and in front of it. His tongue was thick
and his lips cracked lightly as he parted them.
Malcolm managed to reach a hand out of the bag
and pull the wool toque farther down over his
eyes. He breathed deeply again — how much
more could he sleep? — and faded into reverie.

His father's shotgun lay across the bed beside
a Bible. On the floor was a pile of engineering
journals that had not been opened. They were
also his father's, and more than five years old.

"Are you all right?" his mother had called
from the other bedroom where she was lying in
the dark.

And back then, closing his eyes, Malcolm had
tried to relax as he heard her voice, feeling tiny
nerves twitch in his eyeballs, as if he'd been staring at a computer screen much too long. The
jumping was uncanny, the way it was when he'd
first noticed what staring at computers did to his

eyes, an effect different from anything he'd felt before.

"Is anything the matter?"

"No," he'd answered.

She didn't quite say: Don't try to hide anything from me, dear. She had never called him dear, they were too close, and she never came right out and said that kind of thing but oh she had a gift: of phoning if he was away, of calling to him, interrupting him, of talking to him at times like this. He would be in extremis, the phone would ring, and it would be his mother.

Without replying, Malcolm opened his eyes and lifted the gun off the coverlet, checking the magazine to make sure it was empty. Every time he lifted a gun he was surprised at the weight. It seemed, always, a new, shocking sensation: from the first one he had ever held, his dad handing it to him in a yellow field, to this dark, close bedroom.

"Why did Dad leave the shotgun in my closet?" he called back to his mother.

There was a pause. "I didn't know it was there."

He imagined her resting the back of her hand on her forehead.

Gently laying the gun back on the mattress, Malcolm looked at the Bible. Unless he put the book right under the bedside lamp he would be unable to see the print, but he knew what was there, and where it would fall open. An insistent, yawping, relentless energy would rise off its pages, one he had felt so compelled, for so many years, to confront: Paul.

Malcolm pushed the book off the bed. It thumped on the floor, and he thought he heard his mother catch her breath.

As a child he had been told that it was because of Paul that Mother had to wear a hat in church. Hearing that had felt very odd, and he'd been sorry for her; the way he felt when he was sorry for himself.

After growing up, he had gone back to St. Paul and accused.

Well, the Pauls of this world might still be flourishing, but he couldn't fix it anymore; he would have become Paul himself making the effort. And he couldn't fix his mother; how he'd tried.

The causes Malcolm had looked at to explain his generalized anger were vague, shapes passing the cot he had used in his parents' bedroom before he had a room of his own. Some incidents were quite clear — being told his dog had no soul, which meant it was not a sentient being — and he knew whom to blame at different times. He knew the kinds of thinking to blame, the deep-seated assumptions that made people act the way they did. But there was more to it and much had occurred earlier, had swirled and come and gone and had not stopped. Voices without words, agitation, compulsion, how he would react: it had not stopped. His torpor made no difference and his memories turned to formless energy and oppressed him.

The thin, slimy film that clung to his feet, and the realization that he couldn't quite fall back into the morning's stupor, made him open his eyes inside the toque. The light between the wool fibres reminded him how dark his house had been: the kind of darkness it seemed impossible to experience again. He better go outside and see about something to eat. Did extreme conditions require extreme measures? All the bad weather seemed to come from the north-northeast and northwest. When the wind got into that quarter it looked to stay for days. He'd go and look at the sky.

For all his talk Billy was sure his father had never been rain-bound or wind-bound like this. Through all the dark months Big Bill hardly even left the store, staying up late every night, making tea all day and talking to whoever came in.

In spring his father began to go out onto the second-floor porch and look across the empty lots in the sunshine, but when spring was inevitably disappointing, when the gales and freezing rain and April snowstorms came, he'd simply continue winter: the whole quiet, silent town — the little tapestry, the patchwork quilt of streets and bare ground in miles and miles of forest —

so often seemed to be doing nothing but waiting for winter all over again.

In spite of his years in the North, and his talk about actually living there and its being his home, Big Bill hadn't been out in bad weather for days at a time.

Dad would just wait for the next nice moment, the next patch of light, before going back inside.

Where they were now the comfort of hot tea was impossible; these tents were nylon dog hutches in which you could never put a stove. There wasn't any wood; the moss was soaking wet. How different from the Beaulieus' big canvas job; but the Beaulieus, at least the old guy, had lived in the bush most of the year. The survey Billy had been on used a cook tent.

These expeditions of "fly in and float down" always had to do with strangers; even the equipment looked out of place.

Billy pulled the second sleeping bag up over him and used it like a quilt, hoping he could make it cozy. He burrowed in. At least he had a hidey-hole.

There was nothing to read. No wonder his father read so much — the hours would pass slowly by. They'd passed that way before. He was warm.

"Just remember when winter seems too long, and here in Fort Smith we get a lot of winter, it *is* a long time: Go with it! See what a beautiful country this is; love it."

Easy enough to say as you waited for your kid to get home from school so you could have someone to talk to, standing in brilliant February sun that was kept safely outside by a window. Leaning against bins of shiny bolts and screws, or piles of stiff cotton work gloves — tools and clothing he would never use himself — his father would tilt his head provocatively and peer at his son.

"Dad, you never go outside."

"Cloud cover and not the *time* of day dictates when it's warmest and coldest." Through his black beard Big Bill's long, stained teeth grinned. That smile of his was as much a fixture of the store as the hardware.

"Do you actually believe that?" Billy had asked.

"I believe it's the low angle of the sun. I'm doing a pamphlet for the tourist board on our weather."

"Then get out into it!"

"I'm no big fan of winter, kid."

"Don't call me kid."

"But if you resent it you'll get sad. Cabin fever."

"Well, you've got it," Billy had said.

"We get two hundred days a year here when the average daily temperature is below zero degrees centigrade."

"Whoopee shit."

"Don't talk to me that way," his father said, but didn't mean it, he just wanted to keep going.

Billy would leave and go upstairs. "I'm sick of it and I'm getting out of here."

His father would call, "I know what you mean, but don't get down. If you get sad, you'll get worse. Take pleasure in the place. Love it."

Billy was amazed he'd said that. Maybe he really did love it; his mother was always surprised that his father didn't need to "get out" the way she did. But then his father always stayed warm.

Claire stuck her head out of the tent, and the quality of the cold astonished her.

And there he was, down by the water, stalking along with no shirt on. The curve of muscle on his bare back was as tanned as the sand. Khaki pants and long arms made his legs look slight. The restlessness was a strange combination: of weasel-family hunting, a mink working along a shoreline, and the back-and-forth pacing of a captive animal, psychotic from confinement.

She'd seen it in the lab, she'd seen it at the zoo, she'd seen it in the field.

Now he was flexing a bicep and staring down at it, not interested in the tundra or wind; his body, what it could endure, was the universe.

Pathetic. She had to withdraw her head because the cold made her temples ache; the rain felt like sand thrown against her face.

It might have been a habit with her to always pick the wrong kind of man, but she did not want Daryl and never had.

Patience — it wasn't resignation just yet — was one of the things she was good at. Just like getting involved with men who were unavailable. But the intensity of this weather, which filled even relaxing with a little worry, made her wonder just how long she could support the enforced idleness.

They had decided to stay put and not to challenge the environment, as Billy said. But the reassuring things everyone said were full of uneasiness. "Time to lie back and enjoy life," Malcolm and Billy had said to each other. Both of them looked a little furtive as they spoke, as though they were lying.

Thinking about how Daryl had tried to kiss her made her pick at her nails and neglect to get back in the sleeping bag. Moisture spotted the cover and looked about to congeal.

He had made his comment about his marriage and she'd ignored it, getting down to photograph the old toboggan against the grey-green lichen. How sunny that day had been.

As she noted that wood didn't seem to rot or get punky up here, just to turn hard or crumble, and while she was focusing the lens, she had felt breath in her hair. Daryl was beside her, or at least his face was. Then she'd felt his thin lips on hers and his tongue. What amazed her was how he'd gotten himself into position; his head must have swivelled on its socket!

"Stop!" She nearly spit the word out and fell backward.

He did. Of course she had to say it; he hadn't picked up any signals. Even her kneeling down should have let him know she was trying to get away.

"Claire," he said.

"What makes you think you can come on to me?" she'd asked.

"Well…" There was a slow smile, as though he knew better. He was trying to hang on to his confidence.

"It's stupid," she said.

"We're up here. I dunno. My wife…"

"I don't want to hear about your wife!"

"I'm sorry." He obeyed, but with a look of reproach. "Is that all I mean to you?"

"What are you talking about?" she said.

"I thought…"

"We work together. I'm glad you came." She went back to taking her pictures. They had walked to camp in silence.

Now look at him, taking it out on the whole goddamn Arctic. He'd fail in that fight, she thought, surprised at her bitterness.

The wind didn't come through the tent, but still got in. Claire pulled slacks on over long underwear and thought even more bitterly that the idea of using body heat and no clothes to get the most heat in a sleeping bag was wrong, boy was it wrong.

Daryl was so busy. Before the bad weather, on their last day of travel, she had heard him outside at three a.m. The seemingly innocent banging of pots was a signal to them all to get up. An early start that day was meaningless. His clamour implied they had to make time: to where? The rendezvous was well within reach; they could always be found on the river. But as the trip went on Daryl just "decided" to do things at the oddest hours, and whatever Daryl decided to do was different from what Billy and Malcolm thought they should do. They wound up following Daryl. And he did so much work, so much of the heavy lifting, the carrying of canoes. He constantly showed how he could handle two or three heavy packs at once. Now look at him.

Soon he would have an idea to move again, but they wouldn't, they couldn't, in these conditions. But shortly enough the tent would have to come down, and go up, and come down. Curse this pitching.

VIII

"...The Fairest Flower of All the Fields"

The food was floating away. Awash, some packets were still close to shore, their contents of dusty granules clearly visible inside. A few others had come up onto the beach.

"Somebody's crazy," Billy said. "Really crazy." His face twisted as he spoke.

"I'm cold." Claire tucked her fists into the

sleeves of her cardigan. She was simply surprised: that this had happened, and that she felt
so little and so differently from Fort Smith,
from the night of panic and drugs. And she realized she'd forgotten to take any Valium. That
she didn't need to was another small revelation.

"I better get what I can." Daryl walked off to
pick up the flotsam on the beach.

Malcolm watched him go. The sand was
damp and Daryl's footprints deep; behind him
the tundra was brown. Sere and red, Malcolm
thought, dogwood in early spring but with the
darkness of berries. What little greening that
had occurred seemed to have gone. A setback.
Fall, his father, hunting. "We can retrieve more
in a canoe," Malcolm called.

"Come on then." Billy wheeled toward the
canoes beached high above the water line.

On discovering the loss, Malcolm's cry to the
others was faint, just above the wind. Another
day had gone; it was near a rainy supper time.
They had emerged from separate tents to go
and stand on the shore. The sky was low, the

water darker than the darkest lead pencil yet gin clear, strikingly transparent close up.

"I'm cold," Claire said again.

"Go get your rain gear on." Malcolm went after Billy. "We'll go downstream to see what we can find. We'll still have a meal."

But they didn't. There wasn't enough. After they had gathered and sorted what was left on the beach they went back to their tents and Malcolm brought around some raisins and peanuts. "We'll save what we can," he said as he handed the rations in.

Billy proposed someone staying up all night to guard what was left.

"There's no need for that. We'll put what's left in with you. And if it's gone we'll know who did it." Malcolm's laugh was a cackle.

On the surface there was little shock; the loss of so much food didn't seem that unusual. The weather seemed to have silenced everything.

It was decided to have a meeting in the morning, order and ration what was left, then get down to the Thelon and to the first rendezvous

spot and stay put, waiting for the airplane. Whatever personality disorder, as Daryl put it, had
caused someone to act angrily and destructively
seemed matter-of-fact, just more bad luck like
the mix of people and climate; an untimely glitch,
part of a "disastrous" trip.

"There goes the bright idea around this wonderful adventure," Daryl said. "I've viewed more
wildlife on Yonge Street."

"We'll den up," Billy reassured himself. "We'll
be okay."

"We'll find out who did this," Malcolm said.

She had gone to pick berries with Billy.

The morning after the loss of the food they
had packed up and tried to move. There had
been breakfast, the last of the porridge, a package for each, but no powdered milk. The wind
abated but the sky still touched everything with
grey: boulders, lichen, willows, and sand. Colours
that stood out were at the edge of tundra ponds:
mineral-clear water, black in the distance; rusty
moss, sienna.

"When are we going to talk about what we're going to do?" Daryl twisted the cup of hot water he held close to his chest.

"We'll just get to a good spot then wait," Malcolm said.

"But who did this?" Daryl looked up with false good humour.

"We'll just go on for now."

They hadn't gotten anywhere. Paddling against a headwind, even if light, was slow work, but in the blustery death of the gale they could make no headway, a waste of energy to try. So they had to set up camp again in the place they started from. It wasn't as cold, however, and it was possible to do things outside the tents. She had picked Billy as her partner.

They tottered a little as they set out side by side, and Claire felt she was taller than he, that she could lean over against him. Bending down, then straightening up, they seemed to be moving aimlessly, except they were walking away. She could picture the two of them, small figures on the side of a hill.

"There isn't really anything," Billy said. "Just cranberries left from last year. We'll be lucky to get thirteen this morning."

"Overwintered cranberries," Claire said. "Here's one. My God, it's sweet!" She noticed her hands were streaked with black. Was her face? She could not remember the last time she had looked in her little mirror. She felt no urge to do so again soon.

"One," said Billy.

"Not quite like it's been boiled, or out of a jar." Claire didn't know what to do. There was no juice on her fingers but she theatrically sucked them clean. "It's okay."

"There's no berries, really," Billy said. "Nothing till August, and I'm glad it's not August. Snow flurries." He raised his eyebrows and stared right at her.

"This won't last?" she asked. She realized she had never looked at him closely.

"It's summer. It has to change." Billy took his cap off. His hairline, where his darkly greasy hair was pushed back, was white.

"How old are you?" Claire asked.

"Eighteen." His clear skin, and the fact he wasn't big, made him seem younger. "How old are you?"

"Thirty-two," she said. "Let's take a break." Claire dropped down on some sand and gravel behind a small ridge. "It's almost warm down here."

"Yep." He lay down beside her, supporting himself on an elbow. His face was close to hers; he searched the ground. There was a black streak on his throat and she noticed that his cheeks, below the tan, showed a tinge of blood that made them look like ripe plums. It was disturbing, not healthy, like the way his stiff fingers grabbed at the growth near them, closing abruptly, almost greedily, over a small seed. "Got one!" he said.

"Here." She took the berry from him, put it in the container, and covered it carefully with a handkerchief.

"A couple of others and we'll have a rattle," Billy said.

113

"Have you lived here all your life?" she asked.

"Not here!" He lifted his eyebrows and glanced around. "Not really." He looked down and pulled at fine black strands growing in tufts on the gravel. "Pubic hair moss," he said. "Good to start a fire."

They stayed there all the morning, almost warm, cradled in a hollow of sand with purple flowers and the black moss adding colour to their little world. The enormous circumference of the Barrens disappeared. Claire realized how much time she had spent avoiding looking at it; here, everything was comfortably close up.

"Have you lived in Fort Smith all your life?" she asked again.

"It seems that way," he said. "But we're from Alberta. I didn't want to move."

"The last man I lived with was from Alberta," she said.

"What did he do?"

"Kept the TV on all the time."

"No, really."

"Even during meals," she said. "He controlled that remote. He was remote."

"Come on."

"He was a photographer."

Billy's obvious indignation at the way she had
been treated was confusing. Irritably, Claire
wanted to tell him that he couldn't do anything
about it; at the same time she was touched. So
she stretched in front of him, knowing she was
manipulating him by doing it. "Let's get back."
Claire flexed, yawned aggressively, then, as if having second thoughts about what she was doing,
cut herself off with a grunt.

"Like, were you a model?" Billy asked.

"You know what I do."

"I mean it," he said.

"I was in some of his photographs. My girl-
friend and I."

"What kind of photographs?"

"Let's get back."

"To what?" Billy rolled away from Claire and
lay on his back. "We aren't going anywhere
today. My dad always says to lay back and enjoy
life on days like this."

"So I've heard. How long will we have to enjoy life?"

"There's no choice," he said. "But the weather can change quickly. It's changing right now. And we're smart not to try and travel — it's no time to challenge the environment." He pronounced the formula just like Big Bill.

"Really," she said.

"It'll change," he said. "If it was August I'd worry. But it isn't."

"Whatever you're in seems it's always been there and always will be." Claire's voice had gone strangely flat.

"There's brightness behind those clouds," Billy said. "Can't you feel it?"

"Yes." Rolling over on her back, Claire closed her eyes. "But no matter what I wear I always have some kind of chill."

"We're sheltered."

"It's bright behind my eyelids," she said.

Billy didn't answer. She didn't bother to look at him.

"You know, spring never seems to come down

south either," she said. "It's part of being a Canadian."

"Spring?" Billy grunted.

"I mean, in a way there is no spring, is there?" she said.

"Well, there is spring," he said. "And B.C. —"

"Anywhere in the country. Days, months go by, and there's no difference. You go to work, the weather changes, and there's signs, but they don't seem to matter. And it'll get rainy or cold or something again so quickly. You're always surprised and angry yet you shouldn't be. But you're always surprised."

"Summer's nice," Billy said. "I hope we get some. Sometimes summer can skip a year up here."

"It can be too hot where I grew up," she said. "Though that's impossible to believe now."

"I look forward to getting back to summer," Billy said.

"In Fort Smith?" she asked, as if she found it hard to believe not only that Fort Smith had seasons but that anyone could actually live there all year.

"And trees," he said.

"I guess it's like monsoons. Big sweeps of weather with nothing to break it."

"This is the farthest from a monsoon you can get," Billy said. "It's northern."

"Oh, I know." She bit her lip thinking about it. "But it's big change I'm talking about."

"We have still days." Billy turned to look at her but her eyes remained closed: her eyelids were lavender, her skin brown. There was a sheen below her cheekbones.

She's imagining distance, he thought. "Wait'll the bugs come," he said.

"Starvation, after all, is a common enough occurrence in the Far North." Malcolm's palm smoothed the air above packets spread on the ground as if he was conjuring over them.

Billy jammed his hands into his pockets.

"Well let's talk about it then," Daryl said. "Let's have a debate."

"We're certainly far from a test like that." Malcolm spoke mildly.

"This isn't about a test!"

If Malcolm had been holding anything, Daryl would have ripped it away from him, Claire was sure of that. But Malcolm stayed on his knees and returned his attention to the packages of remaining supplies, as if they were alive, as if he were addressing them. "Who decided to put us to the test?"

"You know this isn't any game. There is going to be a lot of discomfort because of what you did," Daryl said.

Malcolm looked up again. "I didn't do it."

Claire half heard him. Her mind felt vacant, as if there was nothing to sharpen it on. She found it difficult to grasp what people were saying.

"This weather is shitty," she said. "Shitty, shitty, shitty."

"There's no guarantees," Billy said.

"What's that supposed to mean?" Daryl was volcanically irritable, but he also looked confused, as if he too was finding it hard to take in what was being said.

"Well, we have berries," she said lightly, "and enough sugar to fix them with."

"Yeah, right," Billy said.

She felt she hated Billy, found herself looking at him with loathing. She surprised herself. "We're hungry," she said to Malcolm.

"Not really." Malcolm didn't look up at her.

"What do you mean, not really!" Daryl spoke so fast it seemed he was about to jump. Claire moved over and stood beside him.

IX

A Gale of Wind

"We're going to have to hunt for food." Malcolm sucked air through his teeth and tucked the shaft of his paddle under his arm, keeping the blade in the water. "No choice." He tilted his head back to rest on his neck, relaxing theatrically, and shut his eyes.

They had reached the Thelon, and held the

canoes side by side while passing around some raisins.

"What crap." Daryl rinsed, dipped, then lifted a cup to drink. A light breeze moved the small flotilla. Malcolm opened his eyes and steered.

"This is big country." Billy looked around.

It was all Claire could think about. Green, rolling tundra didn't come right down to them anymore. The Thelon, where they set out on it, was immensely wide. Far far away was a dark low hill; she was completely aware of it in the landscape. Never had she seen any landform like that swelling rise: ochre lichen mixed with dark grey boulders. Somehow she had expected to see it all her life.

By the shore a golden flank of land shimmered like wind in the fur of an animal.

"Going in." She wasn't sure if she whispered it or said it aloud, a phrase she had heard from one of the others, but being here was exactly what it meant.

Now she imagined voices across the water. People who had been here before. They were in groups; they were laughing, long ago. Then three harsher notes in the enormous quiet, from only decades ago; they sounded as unreasonably joyous as she.

"We are going to have to do something," Malcolm said. Crouched in his khaki work clothes, his face red and his voice breaking, he looked small and old.

"That's ridiculous," Daryl said. "We'll just pull ashore and wait here. This is where we're supposed to be, isn't it?"

"I'm not sure," Billy said.

They made another camp because the weather turned again. It was here, as she stared at the wide body of the Thelon, that Malcolm had come up on her from behind. His concern that she would get wet was only his making a point; his care was a demonstration of superior competence, as was his announcement about a chipping site. It was all about him, and she didn't care.

Away he tramped, short steps, hands in pockets, dramatically presenting his back to her, at
the same time letting her know she'd miss
something. She watched; when he'd reached a
close ridge there was the impression that he was
disappearing into the country. She turned away.

Another gust of rain, a gale of wind, hit her.
She was conscious that the hail-like rattle was
off her body and not the tent. The nature of her
fatigue puzzled her, but in an abstract way. It
was more like languor, and she was sure that, no
matter how difficult things got, she would never
feel as she had in Fort Smith.

Across from her a scud of squall was torn into
spindrift; there was light in it and it was not
winter light. The tundra changed from brown
to gold. Clouds charged over a rise so quickly,
like an army, close to her.

Back in the tent she went to sleep again, and
in the liquid warmth of that sleep wondered if
she could sleep too much. A day and a night?
Her body felt wonderful; her body was everything. Changing into different, but dirty, long

underwear, she looked at her legs, her flat stomach, and felt she was looking at the body of someone else. Oh, it was her, but years ago, so real, so sweet.

As she awoke to the constant light she still heard rain, but saw the tent was not moving. The sound was that of insects' bodies — tiny carapaces, membrane of wing, that which cracked — beating against the nylon. The atmosphere was oppressive. She wasn't sweating so much as oily; there was a scummy film in the corners of her mouth. She would sleep again, but heard someone outside.

"C'mon down," Billy said.

She felt rather than saw his shadow kneeling by the tent flap.

"What's the point?" she murmured, but he didn't hear.

"I'm going to boil up. We'll have afternoon tea!"

He exaggerated, looking for the familiar, looking for comfort too.

"Why don't we just stay put?" She turned

into the damp cotton of her pillowcase. Inside she felt the outline of the folded sweater that served as a pillow. There was a wet oval from where she had slept and she moved her lips away from it.

"The thing to do, when you don't know where you are, or aren't sure, is to *boil up!*" Billy inflected "boil up" in an extreme and corny way but he also sounded serious enough.

"But we know where we are."

"Man —"

"I'm not a man." But he wasn't listening.

"— you know, I get mad at Dad and his bush pilot friends for their advice, but I've heard 'boil up' too often not to try it. Si'down. Be calm. Make tea. Figure out where you are, what you can do."

"I said we know where we are." Sudden worry made her feel nausea, and she sat up. But the attack passed quickly as once again she became aware of the smooth surface of her tummy. "Don't scare me." She ran her hand over it.

"We do," Billy said. "But not in terms of getting a plane in."

Fascinated with the firm feel of her belly, Claire closed her eyes, picturing the colour of her skin: no tan, faded yellow.

"Wait a sec, then," she said.

"Forget the tea." Once more, Malcolm had spread what was left of the food upon the ground and sat beside it.

Each package was nudged with the back of his hand, an imprecise, delicate gesture, as he counted them and told over their names: "Big Bill's Beans, two; peaches-and-cream porridge, three; beef stroganoff, one." His long shin bones made squatting as he did look uncomfortable, but he seemed not to notice.

"You have misled us completely," Daryl said.

Malcolm recounted and itemized under his breath.

"There is a problem with waiting here for an airplane," Billy said. "But it's a good place to wait for other parties to come by. It is a major juncture."

"Who the hell will pass by?" Daryl spoke bitterly.

"Summer travellers, like us." Malcolm looked up mildly.

"We can't count on it," Billy said with finality. "It could be a while. Weeks. You just can't count on it."

"Why not?" Daryl asked.

"That's the blessing of where we are," Malcolm said. "The truth. It's one of the few places on earth where there aren't other people. But there's a trade-off: the silence of God."

"Please," Daryl said. "There'll be other people; there's always other people. This is the twentieth century."

"We should go to where we arranged the rendezvous," Billy said, gulping air before he continued. "Some guys dumped in the Thelon canyon and they were out here over three weeks. They were up against it."

"With what we have we might not get as far as planned," Malcolm told him. "We don't have much."

Daryl grunted.

"We don't," Billy insisted.

"You can romanticize this to hell if you want," Daryl said, "but we're not the Hornby party and we're not Stone Age natives with life-spans of forty. We're not 'overwintering' or 'up against it' or anything romantic and we haven't even seen the goddamn wildlife."

"When we came in we did," Claire said.

Malcolm hissed, "We're going to have to see them again."

"Who's them?" Daryl said, and before Malcolm could respond, "Shove it, please."

"Why don't we do what we planned?" Claire positioned herself beside Daryl again. "No surprises. If we have to say put, stay put." She bit her lip.

"I agree it's best not to wander about when you're lost," Billy said.

"Oh, we're lost, eh?" Daryl said. "Not by my map."

"We know where we are and it isn't the best place for an airplane," Billy said. "It is possible to go on."

"It's exposed here," Malcolm said.

Billy shrugged. "Our tents are pretty good."

"It's windy, unpleasant, and there's nothing around," Malcolm said. "We have to hunt."

"Bullshit," Daryl said. "Cause suffering to harmless animals? *Experiment* with hunting?"

"We can be seen here," Claire said.

"There isn't enough stuff left for three days," Malcolm explained.

"People can go without food a lot longer than that." Claire looked across the river. She was sick of being afraid and wouldn't be anymore.

Malcolm picked up a bag to examine its underside, then put it back down to be poked casually, as if it was entrails, or he was checking to see if it was alive. "Let's make one push, one more effort, to get to the Hornby cabin. It's a spot where every party on this river visits, so we'd have that. It's a known spot, planes overfly it, and it isn't that far."

"Actually, I've heard it's pretty hard to find that cabin," Billy said.

"That's it," Daryl said. "Make it difficult."

"There's shelter there," Billy offered. "Hornby Point."

"Do you think a name makes a difference up here?" Malcolm asked with a spirit of neutral inquiry.

"It's a consolation," Claire said. "Knowing where you are."

"I know where I am," Daryl said.

"Why move then?" Claire asked.

"Something to do," Malcolm said. "Fill the time. More food."

"Fill the time?" Daryl said. "Well, it might not be too good to squat here for three weeks if worst comes to worst. It never hurts to act."

"But in terms of caribou, we're more likely to get the migration here," Billy said.

"The caribou are a myth as far as we are concerned." Daryl's smile was hard, heedless of Billy's age or feelings or position. And he warned him against listening to Malcolm. "They're irrelevant. We're not going to need the caribou. What good'll they do us, except to say we've seen them?"

"They're the point of this trip," Claire said.

"Well," Daryl said, "they're a missing part of the package."

Abruptly, Claire walked back to her tent. The three men didn't move, outlined against the strange, dark water and sky.

Then Daryl and Billy put hands in pockets and turned their backs to the wind. It mussed their hair.

Malcolm remained sitting on lichen that looked sombre and wet.

Billy finally spoke. "Well, if we get there we can hole up. And there's supposed to be game on Grassy Island." He wasn't sure if Malcolm heard him.

The older man got up, joints cracking. He seemed very tall. "The cabin's in a tongue of forest, a grove. The Barrens and forest." Arms behind him, hands in fists, he stretched, then exhaled. "Way out here. Two hundred yards from the forest to the Barrens."

"Billy." In a conciliatory, gentle way, Daryl said the name. "Does it matter if we miss the caribou?"

"Oh, yes. I mean not us, but…"

"What are you worried about?" Malcolm addressed Daryl. "Why are you worried about caribou, about what we'll eat?"

"I'm not talking about that."

"Or shelter, or clothes," Malcolm continued. "We'll be provided for. Like migratory birds. Take the best and get out."

"All I've seen is a Harris sparrow," said Billy.

"We are provided for, aren't we?" Malcolm spoke to Daryl.

"Come on."

"Isn't life more than meat?"

X

This Music Is Not about You

Now he was out of sight and Daryl was conscious, not of the chase, but of his own breathing; his breath in a silence that at last was familiar. The sky was still and grey as the rocks. His breath was everything.

Ahead of him. And the way Billy tilted his head to the side when he ran should have made him move crabwise, but he had gone straight up and over the ridge.

Then there were needles in Daryl's calves, and another sharpness in his hamstring. Though his big quads stretched the khaki across his thighs — it was beginning to irritate him, his pants were too tight — he realized his legs could be delicate. He had to be careful, yet he must continue.

The kid seemed immune to tendinitis, going out ahead like that. Daryl was enraged. "Run him to death," he muttered under his breath, mixing up Billy and the caribou they were chasing. Punish them both: for being young, for tender flesh.

"I don't mean that," he said to himself, but something wasn't fair. Daryl might turn an ankle; he was too strong, his legs too big, his ankles too fine. Or foot-foundered was what he'd become, foot-foundered on the stones. The expression startled him; it had no source.

Goddamn, he had to watch it, and had a glimpse of Billy shuffling in a kind of jog-trot, wearing heavy work boots that should have slowed him down. Did those boots come up high and give him support? An advantage. Daryl felt he was in moccasins.

On dry ground the crunch of lichen was as loud as an explosion; Daryl could not gain, nor contain, his anger.

In favoured pockets of tundra he noticed purple blossoms of bog laurel and lingonberry, white flowers of cloudberry and avens, yellows of cinquefoil. The names, which he'd memorized, weren't important now, and not because he was tired. He didn't care which was which, all those names he had recited to the others, marvelling. Billy hadn't known any of them, only bearberry, kinnikinnick, which, he said, you could smoke in a pinch.

Now the plants compelled his attention and enraged him further. What did it matter?

This indifference made him slow down: dwarf birch, alders, and willow would trip him up anyway. But they were near the shoreline — now it was sedges and grasses, wet spots, that slowed him down and destroyed his balance: tussocks.

He urged himself forward. Low ground was the worst.

To keep himself going, Daryl imagined Billy not as a boy but as a dwarf, all head and torso, short legs and arms. He could not allow himself to be beaten!

Yet this idea to run down a caribou had been Daryl's.

"Well, they'll shoot right over the horizon and disappear and then we'll lose *you*," Malcolm had said. "I'm staying here. Never leave the canoe."

"They can outrun wolves," Billy said. "Easily."

"Even pacing." Malcolm shook his head. "What's called pacing. They go fast."

"You want meat, don't you?" Daryl challenged.

"I didn't say that."

Quickly, Billy addressed Daryl. "You're getting it mixed up with those guys on those big long snowshoes who go after moose. In the wintertime. In the taiga."

"A man can run down a caribou," Daryl affirmed.

"You stalk caribou," Billy said. "They're easily

stalked. Sometimes they're easy to get close to. I've seen them come close. Like at water crossings. All going for the same place."

"Like sheep," Claire said.

"No," Billy said. "But all passing the same spot. And I guess if you were lying in the dwarf birch or something you could reach out and touch one. Then if you had a rock I suppose you could pop one; or a sharp stick like a lance. But the thing to do would be wait for the migration. Then you could slaughter 'em. But who knows where the migration will be? They come and go, who really knows exactly where they'll pass?"

"I remind you this is not spring or fall. It is summer. Seasons matter." Malcolm looked directly at Daryl. "The Beverly herd is in a bleak place close by the northern ocean."

"There's stragglers," Billy said. "It's erratic, but there's caribou around."

"Afraid to try?" Daryl asked.

"Yes, I am afraid to try." Malcolm did not lose patience, as they all expected, but he added, "Oh hell, if you're thinking of hunting-gathering people doing this, like the bushmen who run down giraffe or something, even they wound the quarry first with poison arrows. And it takes days! And woodland people did go after moose, who would break through the snow belly-deep at every step. Very seldom caribou. Man, you just want to show that you can run down a racehorse."

"You're the one who's talked about survival."

"Have I?" Malcolm asked softly.

"And a man *can* outrun a racehorse."

"I don't believe you guys," Claire said. "It never stops."

"It really is getting so we don't have anything to eat," Daryl said.

The explosion came, but only in gesture. As if tossing away something useless, Malcolm threw his arm out.

Claire expected the extreme, the provocative, the absurd; she expected to hear a frustrated "That's it, wipe 'em all out! You think they're stupid so wipe 'em all out."

But Malcolm had continued to speak quietly. "Why do we always have to be greater than, better than, bigger than?" he asked. "We can't stand it if another creature is better than us at something. Always have to kick the ass of something big like a grizzly or a polar bear or a racehorse. It *offends* us if something is bigger than us, better than us at something."

"Like a shark," Claire said.

"Like a shark?" Malcolm tilted his head as he looked at her. "Like a shark. We can't stand it if anything is indifferent to us, if we don't count for it. That's why we hate sharks, and reptiles. We think they look at us but don't see us. We can't stand it."

"No reptiles up here," Billy said. "There are bears, though, and if anybody's going to kick ass, they're the ones going to be doing the ass kicking. And you can't outrun 'em."

Malcolm went on. "We look into a shark's eye, a snake's eye, and say — there's nothing there! What we're astounded at is that *we're* not there. So we say the eye is blank."

"You know, there is an old guy in Fort Smith who ran down a caribou," Billy said to Claire.

"My dad talked to him, in the old folks' home. It's a true story."

No one said anything and Billy continued.

"It was in the thirties, out beyond Snowdrift, broken country, Barrens, and they really didn't have anything to eat. Two families. I don't know what went wrong."

"Starving?" Malcolm asked. "Not here. I thought —"

"I'm telling you," Billy said. "This guy was with his brother and cousin. They saw the tracks and knew they just had to follow them and his brother couldn't keep up. They planted a pole" — Billy swung his arm down in an arc — "and went on."

"They planted him," Daryl said.

"Why a pole?" Malcolm asked Billy, surprising everyone by looking confused.

"To find him," Daryl answered.

"In the spring," Billy finished.

There was a pause.

"Did they make him comfortable?" Claire cried out.

Billy half nodded, implying they had done what they could do.

"Did they make him comfortable?" Claire's voice was a small shriek, quick and sharp against the skyline of empty tundra.

"Oh yes," Malcolm said. "They would have made him comfortable."

"Sixty years later and when that guy told my dad the tears just rolled down his cheeks. Sixty years later and like it was yesterday." Billy tightened his lips.

"Did they get it?" Malcolm asked quietly. "The caribou. They must have."

"I guess so."

"And did they return and find his body?" Claire asked.

"I don't know," Billy said.

Daryl had sighed. "Whatever we do, it's better than doing nothing." He had a curious sensation as he spoke of not being where he was, of the lichen and sand under his feet, of his tan slacks leading down to his boots, of the clouds and of the air itself not being quite real. "We have to do something."

So they had set off on the chase, he and Billy. Claire had called it a track meet.

If the plan was ill conceived — really it was only scouting, for miles around there was nothing to see and there was the danger of being split up — at least it allowed him to move.

And he had set out with such power, leaping over small obstacles, pumping his legs. It was Billy who hustled to keep up. With his energy high, Daryl celebrated — he would even bring in the blood-soaked lichen, he thought, the words having nothing to do with killing an animal.

The surge did not last long; quickly the empty tundra appeared a drab and barren place. But a caribou had appeared on the skyline of an esker. The animal, or light behind it, seemed to shine.

Without even a moment of what Daryl felt should have been shared good feeling, Billy had taken off.

At first Billy at least acknowledged Daryl's presence by letting out a link when he noticed the older man trying to pass. It wasn't much, but connected them. Maybe it only made Billy go faster; he seemed able to keep his pace indefinitely.

Now he dropped down and disappeared more frequently; now he was too far ahead; now the boy was out of sight for good.

His disorganized, stupid, haphazard chase — no skill, no judgement, no planning; a charge like that would have made sense only if there was a herd of animals to confuse — had somehow left Daryl behind.

The approach had been miserably bungled.

Let him go.

Alone, Daryl stopped. Ridge after ridge separated him from everyone. He missed them, but was unconcerned: it was a sentimental feeling; they'd all be together soon. The fragility in his legs disappeared.

Now that he was by himself, and he realized he had not been by himself this whole trip, Daryl grew enthusiastic. Being cut off from the others might cost him his life, but that was only a theory. He knew it would not happen. Covered in perspiration, he started to walk, and as he walked he noticed his sweat felt slippery, not absorbed by his clothes, a way it had never been. And he began to realize that he had never been quite alone like this before.

His breath came back; he laughed. He would go up, way up, to a place where you would want to camp and where you could see all around, where you could see game, and the river, and the tiny tents far behind.

As he climbed, Daryl came suddenly upon a landscape that astonished him. The tundra had never surprised him — he had not known what it would look like, and it had been different than expected, but when he first saw it, when he first was in it, the experience was not like this.

The embankment of the esker he climbed was much higher than usual, and it dropped off into a fairyland. There were tundra ponds below, but aquamarine, turquoise. There was exposed sand and gravel, but the sand was fine as flour beside green vegetation mats. And big trees, scattered, spire-like spruce.

This is where he would come and build a

cabin and wait for the caribou to come through. In springtime, on that isthmus between blue water and green shallows. The cabin would be nearly empty; all that mattered were the rough log walls, and he would be outside.

His friends would come: a few, then in great numbers, indifferent to him, but he would be there in their eyes. Their soft nostrils would know him and not be afraid; a clicking of hooves; the beasts all good.

Creatures of Ice Age winter? Migration? No, just silence again. An insect's hum when they were gone. And always the sun.

"This is where I want to be buried," he said.

XI

Warm at the Bone

As her hands worked inside the body cavity of a musk ox calf, Claire looked up at Daryl and smiled. "I won't need any string to tie off the vent. There aren't any contents in the intestines. Nothing to spoil the meat."

The carcass was splayed on its back as she

kneeled over it. Still feeling inside, she shifted the body. "I can't find the windpipe."

Moving the animal made some of its entrails fall onto the Labrador tea, which Claire was using as a carpet. Daryl could smell the crushed leaves of the plant, a smell he associated with being up here and with the wind. There was no odour from the animal. Its head faced uphill.

"What happened?" Daryl was surprised, but stopped himself asking any more questions. He waited to be asked where he had been and why he had been gone so long.

"If I can find that windpipe I can yank everything out." Claire removed a hand that glistened with transparencies. "It's brand new, see?" She lifted a tiny leg. "The hooves are like jelly."

"Stillborn." Hands in his pockets, Malcolm stood watching. "After you and Billy left we came on a whole herd of them, down by the river. Amazing. Maybe they were resting at midday. A lot of them were lying down. Maybe they were waiting for this one to get up."

"We didn't realize what we were seeing."

Claire paused. "It was a surprise, like noticing a bunch of brown blankets. Then you think it's lichen or something."

"We wound up chasing them through the timber," Malcolm said. "Waving our arms, shouting. And at first the bulls did stay behind until the others got away: the females and young. They didn't form a circle, but the bulls stayed behind."

"Shaking his huge head." Claire reached in again. "And his body tilted down toward us on the riverbank."

"That was one of them," Malcolm added, "just tossing a little, like he was annoyed at flies."

"Why did you chase them?" Daryl asked. "You had no hope of killing one."

"We didn't even think of that," Claire said. "We just did."

"Until we couldn't run anymore and they disappeared, about two hundred yards ahead, into the willows and timber. Disappeared," Malcolm said. "We were all alone."

"I found the baby walking back to the canoes,"

Claire said. "It was so strange chasing them. Exciting, natural, I don't know." She tossed her hair. "Do you have a better knife?"

"It isn't a scalpel." Daryl handed her his sheath knife. "Cut the mesentery and the whole peritoneum will come away."

"I know," she said. "But I can't do it blind. I've got to... There's a ridge." She grimaced as she delved, then gave a reckless tug. Liver and yellow, syrups and crimson; most of the viscera came out. "Get me a stick. And I'll need some kind of clean cloth or something."

Malcolm picked up a piece of driftwood and gave it to her.

"That's too thick." Claire examined the bleached branch she'd been handed, then used it anyway, propping open the chest cavity.

"Now I can clean up," she said. "I'll use toilet paper."

"Don't use it all," Malcolm said.

Standing up stiffly, Claire faced Daryl. She kept his knife, resting the handle on her hip. As Daryl was about to speak she bent over to discover what remained in the small darkness at her feet, what needed to be trimmed and wiped.

"I've got to soak my feet," Daryl said. "They're swollen."

Claire poked at the carcass.

"I should wash them in warm water. They feel honey-combed. Like dirt and gravel are eating into them. They need soaking."

"We don't have anything to soak 'em in," Malcolm said.

"I guess if I keep them dry... Rest will work." Daryl was suddenly very tired.

"You should have seen it! The big shaking head," Claire said. "The size of it, the curve of horn and the hump — all matted. I can't get over it."

"They've been known to charge," Malcolm said.

Claire shuddered a no — charging had not been a consideration. She remembered the bad temper, the eyeball in whose periphery she'd been mirrored. Then the agile turn and quick gallop, long stomach hair sweeping away.

"How do we cook this little guy?" Malcolm asked.

"You'd think there would be more fish up here," Daryl said. "Isn't that how the Indians got along? Fishing was a much bigger component of survival than it's given credit for."

"We get a barbecue and he complains," Claire said.

"But we haven't thought of fishing," Daryl said. "Fish should be plentiful hereabouts."

"In *some* places," Malcolm said, "There aren't a lot of species. They grow slowly. Anyway, what are we going to fish with? And I'll tell you — counting on the Thelon for fish? Like hell."

"There's no fat on them," Claire said. "You can starve on trout."

"Char," Malcolm said. "Grayling."

The one fish she'd seen must have been a lake trout, huge and blue in the water, old. Flesh seemed to hang off it like the tatters of a uniform: bone-head, whale-back, ghoul-mask. At a wide, deep part of the river it had nosed in where a rock wall dropped straight down. Visiting, the apparition touched the shore and left.

154

The calf at her feet would miss what was going to come; summer was so short, although being in it you were sure it would never end. Yet today cloud cover took what was clear out of the water. That close sky rolling over the near hill, the space that seemed imaginary until you climbed up and looked — and still didn't seem real because of the overwhelming necessity to leave it, to get out.

An emptied bundle by her shoes that had never been born; never tested each breath for the peculiar flavour of being alive. Fall, the failing light, would have no effect; it would never miss its mother. How many timeless tundra mornings?

"We need fat," Claire made herself say. "I've craved steak. I've imagined a plane flying in to drop some off. Yet now I'm not too hungry."

"Boiling would be the most efficient," Daryl said. "We'd get all the nutrients."

"Don't you want to suck the sweet grease?" Malcolm asked.

"It's like after you've cleaned fish, you don't

155

feel like eating them." Claire made her explanation sound like a question.

"We've cut down on our intake," Daryl said. "It's bound to have had an effect. I mean, I think about food a lot. Don't we all."

"Charred on the outside, warm on the inside will do for me," Malcolm said. "Let's roast this sucker."

"You prefer it cold at the bone?" Claire asked.

"Let's eat," Malcolm said.

"Its life to help ours," Daryl said.

"Born dead." Claire turned away from him and wiped a hand on her pants. "Would you roast the sucker if it came from a factory farm?"

"I'd roast it if it was road kill." Malcolm picked up the carcass and cradled it in his arms. "We're entitled."

"It's so young," Daryl said. "It's hard to accept in populations but the young often —"

"We'll undress it to dress it." Malcolm cut him off. "You skin them by pulling the hide up and off, just the way you'd lift a sweater off a kid."

"The way you keep telling that story makes

me think you've worked in an abattoir," Daryl said.

"Trapper's technique. I read about it."

"You're an ex-sausage maker."

"No," Malcolm said.

Claire handed Daryl his knife. "I wish Billy was here."

No one answered her, no one offered "He'll be fine." She realized she wasn't worried either.

The two men peeled the hide and jointed the meat. Then they all began to hold small pieces of flesh on sticks over the fire. The small amount of fat that came out was so clear, slightly tinged with a light azure, that Claire wanted to drink it — she'd make a broth, chew any globules there might be to break them down and spit them into the soup.

"It's tender," Daryl said.

"Veal's tender," Claire said.

"The young are delicate food." Malcolm looked at Daryl as he cut some ribs off and put them to the side. "For Billy," he said.

"You know, when you talk like that I can't

help but think you're talking about my kids."
Daryl reached over to cut some ribs of his own,
adding to the small pile.

"I'm not," Malcolm said. "Notice there's no
musk smell."

"Only the males smell," Claire said. "The
older ones."

No one would go to bed, and it was hard not to
eat everything. They argued about the meat.

"If we leave it out something else will come
along and get it," Claire said. "It'll attract bears."

"Better than in your tent." Daryl balanced a
rib on the blade of his knife. He was nearly full.

"Do bears really worry you at this stage?"
Malcolm asked.

"They do," she said.

He shrugged. "All this worry about bears.
People go to a cabin, always worry that a bear'll
come out of the woods. All the busyness, all the
worry. What's really scary is that *nothing* will
come out of the woods."

"What woods?" Daryl said. "The black bear and grizzly are a different animal. They evolved differently."

"It's the same principle in northern British Columbia as here, or anywhere," Malcolm said.

Taking a piece of blackened meat in her hand, Claire made as if to stand up, but then just sat still and bent it back and forth, watching charcoal flake off.

"Nothing is what's going to come," Malcolm said.

Night fell, only a deeper and darker twilight, and they stayed round the blossom of fire. The wind was light, incessant, a small noise near ground. Tents waited in the cottony gloom, but the cold nylon would feel damp. They told themselves they were waiting for Billy.

When he returned, sure enough, they were in the open. From a rising landform Billy looked down.

Still, tiny figures. The black of Claire's hair in

the thick grey light. One toppled over — Claire, holding her side. The others did not move.

Not caring if he was conscious or unconscious, Daryl noticed Claire fall, then returned to his other world — in this state it seemed the real one — going into it as far as he wanted. Androgynous shapes, his wife and children, filled his imagination. Elongated hands, flame-like forms, disturbed and fascinated him. He would never leave them again.

For how long had Malcolm contemplated the head of the musk ox bull that did not charge? Where had he heard that the Jersey bull was the most dangerous animal in the world? As he stared into the coals the individual animal transmogrified into the wild herd, grazing.

The cramp in Claire's side woke her completely. She had to go to the bathroom — the pain with absolute insistence told her she could not. While dozing she'd been enfeebled; now a precise centre, a blockage, a swelling in her lower right quadrant tensed every muscle. Her bowel. Doubling up helped.

Billy came quietly; he could have been travel-ling over snow. She did not hear him, had not sensed him, yet was not surprised to look up and see him leaning over her, supporting himself with a stick.

Curling farther into the foetal position she said, "Something's wrong." The tight core that hurt her was acute, would allow her to move no more, yet she found herself asking, "Where'd you get the cane?"

He kneeled beside her. "Old tent poles. I found them on the Barrens. What'd you eat?"

"Meat."

"We have to clear our systems." Malcolm jerked his head up and addressed the night.

"It's dreadful," Claire said.

"No one can evacuate," Daryl spoke.

Still clutching his staff, using it for support, Billy duck-walked over to examine the offal from the dead calf. He lay the wood down, picked up the stomach, and turned it inside out, into a pouch. "We can put some lights in this. Smoke it. We don't want to waste anything."

161

"I can't shit." Claire's voice was strangled. "Help," she said, her lips dry against the lichen.

"Just sittin' here," Daryl said. "Depressed."

"I don't know how the time passed," Malcolm said.

"Did you find anything?" Daryl asked Billy.

"I can't shit," Claire repeated.

"I was disappointed." Billy let the tripe fall. "C'mon." He cupped his hand under Claire's elbow. "C'mon down to the river."

She curled tighter and felt she was murmuring into a pillow. "What good'll that do?"

"You have to pass it," Billy said. "Even two or three ounces, if you haven't been eating…"

"I can't," she said.

"After fasting the intestinal tract is reluctant," Daryl said. "It's disagreeable."

"It hurts," Billy said.

"The question is, have we really been fasting?" Daryl asked.

"It hurts," Claire said.

"Too much or not enough," Malcolm said. "We've been fasting."

"There isn't anything seriously wrong," Billy spoke to Claire.

"There will be," Malcolm said.

"Shut up," Daryl said.

"There's never been too much," Claire said. "Oh! Help."

"C'mon." Billy softly tugged her sweater.

"Why!"

"It'll be private," he said.

Looking away, Malcolm said, "Either a feast or a famine."

XII

To Make a Camp

Billy was weak, yet he woke very early and made himself pull on his clothes. The weight of a heavy dew was on the tent. It was cold, probably in the forties, and there was more brightness outside than they had yet seen.

This camp was close to where they would have to stay, the place on the map with a name, where anyone travelling on the river would be sure to stop. He unzipped the fly and forced himself out into the morning.

The day was radiant. Across from him was a russet, heath-like space leading to a slope, below a grove that had been occupied before: large trees, a bowl of deep moss with a burned stump. Remains of a winter camp, he thought, in this perfectly protected place. Billy imagined what had gone on there: snow beginning to fall, the howling blackness on the tundra above, still, haunted faces, firelight. A skin being pulled up over shoulders. Those ghosts, what had occurred, was connected with his compulsion to forgo rest and look around. And it was connected with menace.

All this talk of bears. There really was something to be afraid of. He had not mentioned it to the others, but one summer in Fort Smith there had been bears everywhere, in town, all over the place. No one knew why. And they were dangerous. They stalked children. It was no joke.

There was a big one around here. Billy had seen its scat on the ridge trail that paralleled the river, a pile of reddish dung full of the cracked skin of berries. The shape of the animal's intestine was visible on top of the mess: huge. Billy must not wander far. The country had changed since yesterday, become local. A presence lurked.

It was so strange. He knew for certain he would not see the thing he feared, yet nearly all he felt was fear — and wonder. Such clarity.

Once he had crossed the field of sedge, about thirty yards from his tent, and with his pant legs soaked to the knees, he thought about turning back. But Billy went forward; the ground split, a rivulet of mud, a quick, fresh odour. There were trees behind him, and from where he paused colours of sulphur, wintergreen, umber. Willows spread out, as if he was standing in a pond. Now his shoes were wet through. He could see all around: only the shining air. He quit.

Where had their food gone? It seemed there never had been much of it: dried powder, sawdust you couldn't eat. Who wanted to kill them?

167

And they weren't even hungry anymore, at least not all the time. Just weak, and quiet. Then someone would get very angry. But these people erupted even before the food floated away. Once they'd drawn lots for an extra sardine, each person becoming more irritable when something smelled good.

No porridge anymore, no dried milk, no coffee. Nothing. This was the last place on earth where there were no other people, Malcolm had said, they were blessed, the last of their species to experience such landscape. Now all they could do was hope for other people.

The place of graves was not far ahead. A boy his age had died there, leaving a diary. Billy's dad used to rage about the stupidity of the Hornby party, even calling the deaths of Hornby's companions murder. Then he'd admit that John Hornby must have had a passionate sense of the integrity of the country — unlike so many trappers back then: their cabins garbage dumps, just like hunt camps today. Hornby was foolish; but Hornby had an idea for the Thelon Game Sanctuary.

A puckish, elfin man, Billy's father described him, evasive, despairing in his disregard for consequences: oh, what does it matter, Hornby would say. Restless, the way his dad was restless, getting up at two a.m. to make tea, keeping busy, what you did in a small town, or in the North; the bulwark against mental deterioration, getting bushed, cabin fever. Busy as his dad.

Both of them had ideas that put people of his age out here. Irresponsible Hornby — they wouldn't even have a house if Billy's mother wasn't a teacher. "An idiot," his father would say, yet both of them were under the same spell. Hornby travelled; Big Bill never left town. But Big Bill knew so much, though he'd never been near the spot, "the most isolated on earth," that fascinated him. Billy would be there tomorrow. Hornby Point would save them.

Alone, on her knees, her pants done up again, Claire rested in the centre of a bowl of trees. Cachexia was what it was: weakness, poor appetite, alterations in metabolism. All of them were sallow, waxy under the tan, even though they'd been outdoors for weeks. Each day she seemed to tighten another notch in her belt. Clothes were loose on everyone. She liked it.

Picking through the carpet of vegetation, as if searching for scraps, as if she had nothing better to do, she suddenly curled her fingers into a piece of moss and tore it up. Spongy, unnatural-ly green. She held it to the sun: the cap seemed irradiated, phosphorescent. The structures below drew the unnatural colour away; there was dirt. Moss was just moss.

Claire was gaunt, and felt beautiful, even if she was thin as a rake around her rump. Muscle tissue wasted, clothes hung gracefully off your body. They all walked as if their joints jerked in and out of position instead of smoothly, and they were kind to each other. Then someone would get so grumpy, but it didn't seem real. Having to eat was only an idea — it dominated their lives, but was only an idea.

There was movement at the edge of the trees, a shadow as big as a haystack.

Billy was beside her.

"There's a grizzly around here," he said.

"I'm still sick," she said.

"It's terrible," he said. "It's like all of us are clogged up with pounded bones. It's so painful."

"Did you think it would get this serious?" she asked.

"Claire," he sighed, and knelt.

"Did you?" she asked.

"We'll get out of here okay," he said. "But everything disappeared so fast."

"And?"

"We won't have to eat tree bark or caribou dung. Maybe a bit of leather." He smiled.

"Really?"

"If we just get to Hornby Point we can den up and stay still, no problem. You can go without food a long time. I won't have to eat you."

"Nothing like that would ever happen," she said. "No matter what."

"No," he said. "Hey."

"It would never come to that."

"It never would," he agreed.

"Dehydration is what is really bad," she said. "It lessens consciousness, makes you sleepy. Takes away pain."

"Good." He smiled again.

"There's a lot of water," she said.

Suddenly tired, Billy wanted to go back to bed. "Let's get ready," he said.

The presence, peat coloured now, moved in the shadows of the trees. Billy jerked his head up. "Did you see it?"

Claire didn't answer, and didn't move. The sun went behind a cloud.

"Hornby's people weren't cannibals," Billy said. "They treated each other decently."

"Why wait there?" she asked.

Billy put his hands on her shoulders and squeezed. "It's known. We'll be found."

"A syringe of soap and hot water would help," she said. "We have to do something."

"I don't know," he said. "Could we rig one up?"

"There's nothing to unplug. I don't know." Her hair shook.

"We'll desecrate a historical site when we get

172

there. That'll make Malcolm happy. We'll pitch our tents in the ruined cabin and burn —"

"We won't have to do that," she said.

"I know," he said. "Let's go. I'll help you pack."

"You're so thin," she said.

"Jesus H. Christ." Malcolm was already pulling a canoe to the water as Billy, Claire, and Daryl converged on him. Dark metal in clouds that now touched the sun made it colder. The timbered cleft that protected them was enclosed by a high contour upstream and by a ridge. There were pink boulders and red soil, toppled trees and ice damage. "I'm tired." Malcolm stopped what he was doing, rested his hands on the gunnels, and bent forward.

"There's a big bear around here," Billy told him. "I don't like being on the same side of the river as that bugger."

"No bear's going to hurt anybody," Malcolm said.

"Look —"

"Let's get going," Daryl cut in. "I almost said

let's not have breakfast, let's just go." He smiled. "Sometimes I'm not as hungry as I should be. Sometimes I'm ravenous."

Claire crossed her arms.

"We have the current." Malcolm said. "Look at it go. Even with a headwind we'll be fine. I bet you could do thirty miles, forty miles a day with that current."

They all felt a breeze. The wind was starting.

"How far is it?" Daryl asked.

"Not that far," Malcolm said.

"That's a help," Daryl said.

"Okay, twenty clicks, maybe sixteen miles. Something like that. About that."

"How'll we know when we're there? There isn't going to be any sign," Daryl said.

"We should see the cabin from the river."

"It could easily be out of sight," Billy said. "They died in the twenties. There won't be much left."

"There's a bend in the river," Malcolm said. "We'll get out and walk along. The cabin'll just confirm things."

"If we can't find it, how will anyone find us?" Daryl said.

"We're not even there and he says we won't find it," Malcolm talked to himself, then addressed Daryl. "Okay, we don't find it, but we'll be close. There's timber, we'll fell trees. Just being close will be okay. It's not the widest part of the river."

"You'd cut down the trees that take so long to grow?" Daryl didn't speak to Malcolm, just compulsively challenged him.

"Of course," Malcolm said.

"We'll find the remains of the cabin." Billy lifted some lichen with the toe of his boot, then stepped on it. "We can't go further anyway."

"You get so unbelievably hungry, eh?" Daryl said. "Then nothing."

Malcolm looked around. "I hate to leave this refuge, but it's too hidden. We have to go to where we can be seen, and make an impact. An oasis."

"The whole Thelon's an oasis," Billy said.

"There might be caribou wandering around," Malcolm went on.

"What kind of myth is that?" Daryl said.

Billy gestured at the north. "Most of the herd will be between here and the Back River now. But if we're stuck long enough they might come by."

"Or might not." Claire tightened her lips.

"Two hundred thousand of them," Billy said.

Daryl nodded, confirming something. "We won't be there that long. We'll be overdue long before that."

"We could miss them," Claire said.

"The caribou don't matter." Daryl was impatient. "And no Indians are going to show up and rescue us: if they did they'd be on ATVs. We don't need caribou. We need a goddamn plane and there'll be one here in about a week."

"Sometimes no one shows up," Malcolm said. "No caribou, no Indians. The Indians didn't get this far up in historic times, and the Inuit didn't get down. It's far."

"It would be nice to have caribou around." Claire's eyes were bright.

"What for?" Daryl said. "For company?"

"We might get one." Her face was open as she looked directly at him.

"Oh Jesus," Daryl said.

"Let's hope," Malcolm said.

"Our *hope* is that there's a horizontal control point on one of the hills," Daryl said. "And the fact that this place has been surveyed."

"How do you know?" Malcolm asked.

"I saw the marker when I was chasing god-damn caribou. Quit trying to scare everybody!" Daryl started toward Malcolm. "You threw our food away and now..."

Claire drew in her breath.

"No." Malcolm didn't move.

Daryl stopped. "There's always been people on this continent. Everywhere."

"Does thinking that make you feel better?" Malcolm asked.

"There's nobody," Claire said. "Nobody out here."

"We should get going," Billy said. "There's that wind warning us to get out of here."

"What do caribou have to do with us?" Daryl asked.

"Caribou have always mattered," Malcolm

177

answered. "The immemorial custom of the North."

"Bullshit," Daryl said softly. "In our situation we've got to take it easy. Get to Hornby Point, get some trees down like you say, get signal fires ready, take it easy. We're not starving, but we've got to take it easy."

"Okay." Malcolm hauled on the canoe and the keel grated like a sledge over gravel. "I can't get it up."

"Here." Daryl went to help him.

"If some come around it'll be okay," Billy said. "I wouldn't mind. My dad says you get away from the Indians or the caribou and you'll die like a rat."

XIII

"... The Wandering of Desire"

The interior was open to the sky, filled with wood debris and willow; clearing it out for shelter would have been destructive and pointless. Hornby's structure had been derelict for years. They all pitched nearby, at a distance from this locus they had found and from each other.

Before unpacking his own tent, Maclolm had

spent a long time standing beside the cabin. He told himself he was simply without the energy to set up right away. Yet if weak and immobile, he was also compelled.

There was a window and they had used the shelter of the hill to make the building a partial dugout: protection against the north. In one corner was a bent sheet of rust. Was that the remains of the stove that had stood in the centre of the room and on which the paper with the words "WHO LOOK IN STOVE" had been found? In its ashes were the farewell notes, the diary, Hornby's will.

Some of the logs had flaking bark on them; some had split with dry rot. The earth was ochre, and in the graves the bones would surely be brown. They had been skeletons when found, dressed in sweaters and khaki and long underwear; flannel trousers and winter moccasins and puttees. They'd been skeletal living. The boy'd worn a muffler and had pulled two red Hudson's Bay blankets over his head before he died. The silent bodies and the dank interior: pots and

pans with bones in them, the floor all torn up
for firewood, a cluttered table with cups and
saucers, papers and ammunition, plates with
bones. Mouldy clothes in a trunk, a sodden suit-
case, a piece of quartz wrapped in an old sock.
No food. The police had come in the rain.

Once he was in his own tent Malcolm did not
want to go outside again. With this wind and
temperature there could even be snow. The fab-
ric walls ballooned as it was; the shoulder of hill
did little to stop the frame from rocking. The
Barrens would be much worse, though even the
parklike taiga had its terrors — he was invited
to walk on and on, trails led everywhere, the
going was so easy, on and on and on.

Sleep now seemed something ominous, but
he slept, shivery, drooling onto the folded wool
shirt that served as a pillow. And he lay for hours
in the grey light that never changed from morning till night. He only got out of the pile of
clothing that covered him to relieve himself, still
not going outside.

It was always fall here, Malcolm felt, a

promise of worse to come. The cabin site was a still centre in spite of the wind. He would go and look at it again, later — an unresponsive cavity, but it howled.

They had to be safe now. This place could have been so very easy to miss, and they had not missed it. They had scoured the willow along the water for at least a mile before Daryl saw some stumps up in the trees, stumps high off the ground indicating poor axemanship. And grey woodchips. The canoes had been hauled out and overturned at the edge of the river; surely they were visible. A plane could land in here, it must be deep enough. Malcolm would lie quietly and listen.

This was the country that was supposed to be without time, and he had experienced that, no days, only the peace of doing, simply doing. Now it was like the worst Sunday of his childhood, boredom and anxiety. But those dull afternoons thirty years ago had never held such anxiety as this.

Half-conscious, amazed at his own depression,

Malcolm shifted, his foot knocking a pan of excreta that he had covered and put near the door of his tent.

This was simply not possible in North America, anywhere in the world, Daryl thought. No other people! More people were being born every day than had been alive in all of human history. Yet they were alone.

And the wind; the fresh indifferent air. For Daryl time was just like it was at home, time passing. Morning into evening. Too quickly. Light to darkness, even if it was always light. But he began to suspect that the changes, the days, didn't mean anything. Nothing happened. He dry heaved and sat up. Sick. The sky-blue roof of his tent lost colour as it surged with a gust.

There was a noise outside his tent, a noise that was not timeless or of the wind.

"Hello!" he yelled.

"It's me."

Claire, he thought with gratitude and disgust.

183

He felt like asking her if she had an appointment. Sick of her, angry at her, with nothing more to say, he was glad she was there. Being irritated was strange comfort; it disturbed the changeless day.

"Hello!" he shouted heartily, as if hailing someone, though he hardly had the energy to move.

"I'm sorry I threw the food away," she said.

"What!"

"I've apologized to everyone," she said. "I thought we'd lose weight. I was sick of…men. Sick of…"

"Hold on. Just a minute. It's okay. Hold on."

"Well, we'll have to do something" was what Billy said when she told him. Just like Daryl he crawled out of his tent to confront her. Emerging on his knees, Billy looked up to see Daryl and Malcolm coming downhill, converging on them. Claire stood off to the side.

Billy squatted to zip the tent back up, and focused on the tearing sound of the zipper. Any sound that wasn't natural, that didn't belong, helped. Then he stood up.

How gaunt they all were. Daryl had lost muscle mass, was still compact but seemed taller. Malcolm's shoulders looked wider, his neck thinner. It was as if he'd had baby fat on him before, which had softened his outline. Spectres, coming through the trees.

"The wind keeps the bugs down," Daryl barked, in a hoarse voice that did not seem to come from his body.

Malcolm nodded, pop-eyed, glancing around.

"We should make one last try for meat," Billy said.

"It can't hurt," Malcolm said. "If you'll go."

"Why should he go?" Claire asked.

"One last try?" Daryl said. "What are you talking about?"

No one responded. It was cloudy. There was a swirl, a squall with tiny flakes in it, in the circle between them. Where they stood the lichen was the colour of the sky.

"Why did you throw that stuff away?" Daryl finally said it.

Claire picked at her bangs.

Daryl turned to Malcolm. "You don't give a shit about animals now, do you? One last try for meat."

"I do," Malcolm said, seeming to come back to himself. "More than ever," he added.

"Now we have to kill some," Daryl said.

"Do you think we will?" Malcolm asked gently. "Let's go up to the Barrens and see what's out there."

"We'll be near the horizontal control point," Daryl said. "Maybe we'll see something."

"I didn't mean for so much to get lost," Claire explained.

"It's where their lookout was," Malcolm said.

"Only bones by now." Malcolm gestured as they passed the three graves.

"If that," Daryl said.

"Things do decay slowly here," Malcolm argued. He stopped and touched the cross with the initials "E.C." carved into it. "Not a shred of clothing. Not much left."

"This would be a lonely place to die." Daryl said.

"How is it different than anywhere else?" Billy asked.

"We know the names," Daryl said.

"You're dead, you're dead," Billy said. "Other people got in trouble out here. Some died. Lots made it. For a long time."

"You really think there's been a lot of people out here?" Malcolm asked. "Does it feel that way? It's haunted. But not the way we're used to. There aren't a lot of voices, or at least ones we're used to. Not a lot."

"It's noisy enough," Daryl said.

"Oh no," Malcolm said.

"Hard to accept." Claire brushed hair away from her face.

"It's normal," Billy said. "Come on." He had more energy than any of them. Claire took a step forward to stand beside him.

Billy shuddered as she came close. He didn't move.

"Even with that wind it is monotonous silence," Daryl said. "Okay."

"Just quiet," Malcolm said.

Claire smiled at Daryl. "You can talk to me."

"What a desolate piece of real estate," Daryl said, surprised as always at how she continued to make him feel. "Imagine being by yourself!" What enthusiasm she could create. He confusedly felt he loved her.

"If there were some birds, anything around, we'd feel better," Malcolm said.

"Keeps the bugs down." Billy walked away.

"Wait." Claire followed him.

"Dope," Daryl muttered, looking at the bark of a tree. The affection drained out of him; resentment rushed in.

"What's that?" Malcolm flared.

"No, no." Daryl jerked his head, indicating Claire.

"Who do you think you are?" Malcolm looked at Daryl as if he'd never seen him before. His feelings were so intense they seemed to leap from his breast right into Daryl's face.

"Now we'll have to live on aspirin and tea." Daryl shrugged and smiled. Because Malcolm was farther up, Daryl had to tilt his head back to address him. "There's been a lot of mistakes."

Suddenly restless and distracted, Malcolm went forward, catching Billy and Claire at the edge of the treeline. With a loose-wristed, freckled hand Malcolm brushed off his pant legs, though there was nothing on them. Daryl joined them. As they all stared across the tundra Malcolm kept up his aimless dusting, never still, never finishing.

"Stop it," Claire said.

Malcolm let his hand drop.

"There it is." Daryl indicated a ridge, gold against the skyline.

"It's farther away than it looks," Billy said. "I'll go."

"Their ridge," Malcolm said. "Another ridge."

"Yep," Daryl said.

"There's nothing moving," Malcolm said. "There's nothing out there."

"That's the hill they used to look for game," Billy said.

"Look what good it did," Daryl said.

"I'll take a look," Billy said.

"Better den up." Malcolm started at his pants again.

"I'll go." Billy repeated. "There could be that marker on it."

Malcolm swiped at his leg. "What does it matter?"

"Your attitude is worse than throwing the food away." Daryl said.

"Oh." Malcolm slapped his thigh and faced Daryl.

"No one has to go." Claire reached over to stop Malcolm's hand. "There's no need."

"We're in bad condition." Billy smiled. "We stink."

"I can't smell anything," Daryl said. "And I'm downwind from you."

"All I can smell is the cold," Malcolm said.

Claire peered at him. "Your nose is red."

"I'd really like to go home," Daryl said.

"We all would," Malcolm said.

"There is no need to go out there," Claire said. "We're out of the wind now."

Daryl turned away, going downhill by himself. The silence behind the outlandish roaring of the wind, the silence that had frightened him and made him homesick, enfolded him like wings.

XIV

The Country of the Musk Ox in Summer

No one emerged from the small blue tents in the timber. On the tundra behind no solitary animals wandered — to see them would have been a blessing and consolation. That year the great herd crossed the Thelon near the Hanbury; no one was present to watch. The musk ox disappeared, not to be seen again.

The barren ground of northern Canada is a country of winter. But summer — insects, water, the light at the edge of tundra ponds — allows its space and silences, its ringing air so full of life, to be seen in the clearest of ways. To say it is only a country of winter is to be bitter and to deny.

In the place where the little band waited there was no ice; water ran. They waited.

August arrived. In Toronto it was gloomy, specks in the oily rain, traffic worse than usual. Of this weather those in the North felt nothing; in the laboratory where Claire and Daryl worked, the creatures they had handled, those still alive, knew nothing of weather anywhere. They nudged woodchips and had red eyes.

At Fort Smith, Big Bill paced more than usual, thinking about his son, not seeing the summer, uneasy with the change of seasons.

Daryl's children missed him, his colleagues worked out; Claire's mother started to get dizzy spells. The people who knew Malcolm were not worried.

Near the bend in the river no one came, but crosses of split and silvered wood were illuminated by sunlight; the wind died.